DANNY DUNN, SCIENTIFIC DETECTIVE

DANNY DUNN, SCIENTIFIC DETECTIVE

by Jay Williams and Raymond Abrashkin

illustrated by Paul Sagsoorian

McGRAW-HILL BOOK COMPANY

New York • St. Louis • San Francisco • Montreal • Toronto

Also by Jay Williams and Raymond Abrashkin

DANNY DUNN AND THE ANTI-GRAVITY PAINT
DANNY DUNN AND THE AUTOMATIC HOUSE
DANNY DUNN AND THE FOSSIL CAVE
DANNY DUNN AND THE HEAT RAY
DANNY DUNN AND THE HOMEWORK MACHINE
DANNY DUNN ON A DESERT ISLAND
DANNY DUNN ON THE OCEAN FLOOR
DANNY DUNN AND THE WEATHER MACHINE
DANNY DUNN, TIME TRAVELER
DANNY DUNN AND THE VOICE FROM SPACE
DANNY DUNN AND THE SMALLIFYING MACHINE
DANNY DUNN AND THE SWAMP MONSTER
DANNY DUNN, INVISIBLE BOY

Library of Congress Cataloging in Publication Data

Williams, Jay, date
    Danny Dunn, scientific detective.

    SUMMARY: Danny Dunn tries to track down the miss-
ing manager of the local department store with the
aid of a bloodhound robot.
    [1. Science fiction] I. Abrashkin, Raymond,
1911-1960, joint author. II. Sagsoorian, Paul.
III. Title.
PZ7.W666Dat   [Fic]   75-10826
ISBN 0-07-070548-8
ISBN 0-07-070549-6 lib. bdg.

123456789 MUBP 7898765

Contents

1 The Ghost-Finder 7

2 The Man Who Couldn't Decide 19

3 An Unusual Request 32

4 "Fee Fi Fo Fum!" 47

5 A Disappearance 62

6 "It Could Be a Clue!" 75

7 Bleeper the Bloodhound 91

8 More Theories 106

9 The Ragged Man 119

10 Mr. String's Secret 128

11 A Last Chance 141

12 The Triumph of the Scientific
Method 158

ONE

The Ghost-Finder

The tall, gray house on Beckforth Street stood alone in a field of weeds as if its neighbors wanted nothing to do with it. It looked at the street through empty, dusty windows, and Joe Pearson, standing in front of it, found himself shivering in spite of the warm spring sunshine.

"It's like some old skull with blank eyes," he grumbled. "I wonder where Danny is?"

"He'll be here soon," said Irene Miller. She was a pretty girl with merry blue eyes, and brown hair gathered into a ponytail. "I see what you mean about the house. Ugh! I wish you hadn't said that."

"Why did he want to meet us here?" Joe complained. "All he'd tell me was that he had a great new idea."

"That's what he told me. He said it was something that would make us famous."

Joe eyed the empty house. Its paint was peeling, and some of the clapboard siding had split and was falling away from the walls. The roof showed gaping holes where shingles had blown away.

"I know Danny's ideas," Joe said sourly. "Make us famous? What they'll make us is white-haired before we're even old enough to graduate from high school. Nothing but trouble!"

He broke off. Some distance away along the street, a sturdy red-haired boy appeared, pulling a metal delivery wagon behind him.

"Here comes Dan now," said Irene. "What's he got with him?"

As Danny came closer, they could see that there was a small black box in the wagon.

"Hi!" he called. "Sorry I took so long, but

I found this was too heavy to carry all the way here so I had to borrow the wagon from little Harry Burstein across the street from us."

Joe bent forward to examine the black box. "What is it?" he asked.

"It's a radiometer," Irene said, before Dan could answer.

Joe nodded. "I should know better than to ask foolish questions, but here's another: What is it?"

Danny grinned fondly at his friend. The thin, sad-looking boy was good in such subjects as history or English, but he knew very little about science or engineering, fields in which both Danny and Irene excelled. Dan's father had died when the boy was very young, and Mrs. Dunn had taken the job of housekeeper to the famous inventor, Professor Euclid Bullfinch. The professor had loved the boy as if he were his own son, and Dan had grown up in an atmosphere of scientific investigation. As for Irene, who lived next door to him, her father was an astronomer, and Irene had long been determined to become a physicist when she grew up.

Danny said, "It's an instrument for

detecting whether or not there is radiation in a certain spot."

"Like a Geiger counter," Joe said, trying to look as if he understood.

"Something like that. Actually, it measures the temperature of any surface. See this ground-glass screen? It'll show cool places as dark spots and hot places as light spots. So, for instance, if I wanted to check a high-tension electrical cable for leakages, I'd use the radiometer, and a bad splice would show up light, as a hot spot."

"But why did you ask us to meet you here?" said Joe. "There aren't any electrical cables in this deserted house, are there? And even if there were, what's the point of detecting them?"

"That isn't what we're going to find," Danny replied. "I told you I had a great idea. We're going to be detectives, and what we're going to find is a ghost."

"In there?" said Joe. "What do you mean—*we*? You mean you and Irene. Good-bye."

"Is this the fearless Joe Pearson I've heard so much about?" said Danny.

"No, it isn't. This is Joe Pearson, the Youthful Jellyfish."

"I thought writers were always looking for new experiences."

"Oh, don't mind him, Danny," Irene put in. "You know he'll come along in the end. He just likes making a fuss. Go on. Tell us your idea. It sounds very exciting."

Danny picked up the radiometer and slung it over his shoulder by its carrying strap. He started toward the empty house, explaining as he went, the other two following close behind.

"You see," he said, "the big problems about finding a ghost are that it may be invisible and that you can't touch it. But you ought to be able to measure it. There's one thing that always seems to be true about ghosts if you read ghost stories, and that is that whenever a ghost appears people feel a chill. Right? A kind of cold breeze—"

"Stop, will you?" Joe begged. "I'm feeling goose flesh right now."

"Okay, but if that's so about feeling a chill," Danny went on, "it means that something must be converting the heat from your body into another kind of energy—a ghostly energy. Now, you know a certain amount of heat is equivalent to a given amount of energy—"

"The first law of thermodynamics," said Irene.

"That's it. Everybody's always said this old house is haunted. If it is, we ought to be able to pinpoint the source of energy—that is, the ghost—because if we feel that chill, we'll be able to find a hot spot somewhere in the air, and *that* will be the ghost."

"Marvelous!" Irene exclaimed. "It just might work."

"I'll be happier if it doesn't," mumbled Joe.

Danny tried the front door. The lock had long since been broken, and the door swung open with a dismal screech. Danny stepped boldly inside and then paused. Even he was daunted by the gloomy atmosphere of the place.

He was in a small entrance hall which opened into a large living room. The windows were so thickly coated with grime that what little light came in was gray, as if all the

12

sun had been strained out of it. The room was empty, except for a broken chair and a squashed cardboard box. A narrow staircase, its bannister sagging, ascended to the upper floors. From the ceiling hung black rags of cobwebs.

Irene pushed past Danny. "It needs a good cleaning," she said firmly. "Come on in, Joe. I want to close the door."

"I don't think that's such a good idea," Joe objected. "We might want to get out in a hurry."

"If there is a ghost here, it'll never show itself with the front door wide open and sunlight pouring in."

Joe moved, with a sigh, and Irene shut the door. The silence of the house surrounded them and pressed down on them, so that they could hear the pulses beating in their ears.

"What now?" Irene said, almost in a whisper.

Danny snapped on the radiometer. "I guess we'd better just walk around slowly," he said, "until we feel a cold breeze or something like that."

They moved through the living room, along a passage into what might once have been a dining room, with a chandelier that looked as if it were made of dust. They went on into the kitchen and then into a pantry with boarded-up windows.

"I never heard of a ghost in a pantry," said Irene.

They retraced their steps. On the other side of the living room there was a small den lined with empty bookshelves, but on one of them was a mouse nest of paper and bits of wool. Then a long room looking into the ruin of a garden, overrun with thistles, milkweed, and mullein.

"I haven't felt a chill yet," said Dan, shaking his head in disappointment. "Just the ordinary shivers from the creepiness of the place."

"Let's try upstairs," Irene suggested.

They climbed the creaking staircase to a landing, off which half a dozen doors opened into bedrooms and a large bathroom. They entered one of the rooms which looked toward the back of the house. It had only one window, and that was partly blocked by a

14

piece of cardboard covering a broken pane of glass. Danny tried a door in a corner and found that it led to another bedroom. He entered it. It, too, had one dirty window with a crooked shade pulled halfway down. An iron cot with a stained mattress stood under the window.

"Look at this," he said in a low voice.

He pointed at the floor. A large, dark stain could be seen on the bare wood.

"Blood!" said Joe. "Somebody was murdered here."

They crowded around, staring at the stain. Danny felt the hair rise on his neck. He swung the nozzle of the radiometer in an arc, hopefully watching its screen.

As he did so, Irene caught his arm. "Listen," she said in his ear, in a frightened whisper.

Danny cocked his head. Was there a noise, or had Irene only imagined it? Yes—definitely—from somewhere in the house came a faint creaking as of a floorboard under a light footstep.

Dan glanced at Joe. It was obvious that

the other boy had heard it as well. There it came again, this time from the stairway.

The three young people shrank together. Danny felt as if he had turned into an ear. Unconsciously, his mouth dropped open as if that would help him listen.

Someone—or something—was coming up the stairs.

A slight breeze stirred against Dan's cheek, coming from the open door to the other bedroom. His hand was shaking so that he could barely lift the nozzle of the radiometer. He glanced at the screen, but it was still blank.

Irene's grip on his arm tightened spasmodically. He heard Joe suck in a breath. He raised his eyes from the screen.

In the doorway to the other bedroom loomed a giant, dark figure.

TWO

The Man Who Couldn't Decide

"What are you kids doing in here?" the figure said, in a voice like the low notes of a cello.

"You're alive?" Danny blurted, before he could stop himself.

They could see, now that their first fright had passed, that it was a burly man, very broad in the chest and shoulders. His skin was the color and texture of rich chocolate icing. The soft black hat and dark suit he wore gave him a sinister look.

He said, slowly, "Are you trying to be funny, boy?"

"N-n-no, sir," Danny said, wondering frantically how they could get away. With the weight of the radiometer to contend with, he couldn't possibly run down those stairs fast enough—

Irene was saying, "Please don't be angry.

We weren't doing anything. We were just looking for ghosts."

"Looking for—!" The big man pushed his hat back from his forehead and stared at them.

"It's a scientific experiment," Danny stammered. "We're sorry if this is your house. Just let us go and we won't do it again."

The man began to shake, and the three friends drew back in alarm. Strange noises were coming from him. Then he threw back his head and began roaring with laughter. So infectious was the sound that the young people slowly lost their fear, began to smile, and soon were laughing, too, without being quite sure why.

"Looking for ghosts," gasped the man. "Won't do it again! And I thought I had a trio of arsonists on my hands."

He took off his hat and wiped his eyes with enormous, square-tipped fingers.

"But if this is your house," said Danny, "why is it empty? And why should you think we'd set fire to it?"

The man put his hat on again. He reached into a pocket and took out a leather

folder. He opened it and held it out to them. Pinned inside it was a gold badge, around the edge of which were engraved the words, *Detective. Midston Police Department.* Next to the badge was a photograph and the name *Carl Ellison.*

"You're a detective!" said Joe. "I thought you were a gangster."

"Well," said Mr. Ellison, "it shows you you can't judge by appearances. I didn't think much of you, either. I've been keeping an eye on this house, because some of the neighbors saw lights in it one night last week, and when we investigated, we found that someone had spilled kerosene on the floor up here. You can still see the stain there."

Joe looked wistfully at it. "So much for a perfectly good murder story," he muttered. "There goes my bloodstain."

Mr. Ellison chuckled. "No, not murder, but maybe the owner of the house trying to burn it down for the insurance. Or maybe kids up to mischief. We didn't know. So, when I saw you going in with what looked like a container of some kind, I thought I'd just check. What is that thing, anyway?" he added curiously.

Danny quickly explained what the radiometer was and how they had hoped to use it.

"Hm," Mr. Ellison said, in an admiring tone. "Pretty smart. It might work, too. That is, if there are any such things as ghosts, which I must admit I doubt. You haven't had any luck with it, have you?"

"Not yet," Danny confessed. "Maybe we ought to try it at midnight."

"Not in this house," said Mr. Ellison. "Sorry, but it *is* private property, you know. I'm afraid you'll have to leave."

He stepped aside and the three friends went to the stairs. Irene started down, and Dan, glancing back at the room they had left, said, "I can tell you one thing, Mr. Ellison. Nobody was *trying* to burn this house down."

The detective stopped him with one large hand. "What do you mean? How do you know that?"

"Logic," said Danny. "You said the neighbors saw lights up here. If the owner, or anyone else, had been planning to burn the place down, they wouldn't have let anyone see any light. They'd have done it as secretly as they could."

"Good thinking," Mr. Ellison said. "Anything else?"

"Well, a fire burns upward following the air currents. So if I wanted to burn a house down, I'd start from the bottom, not the top."

"Uh-huh. Then why pour kerosene all over the place up here?"

"I don't know. Maybe somebody was looking around with a lantern and it went out. They might have tried to fill it again and in the dark spilled the stuff."

"You ought to be a detective," said Mr.

Ellison. "That's sharp reasoning. I'll have to think about it. Maybe you've given me a lead."

They trooped down the stairs and out into the sunlight. They stood blinking for a minute or two, after the gloom of the house.

Mr. Ellison said, "What's your name?"

"I'm Danny Dunn. This is Irene Miller and that's Joe Pearson."

"Glad to meet you," said Mr. Ellison solemnly. "Tell you what, let me have your address, and if I hear about any ghosts or hauntings, I'll let you know and you can try your machine on them."

"You mean people would report ghosts to the police?"

"We get all kinds of peculiar calls," said the detective. "We had a poltergeist over on Hatfield Road last year, but it turned out to be a faulty valve in the hot-water heater."

Danny gave him his address, and Mr. Ellison said, "That's Professor Bullfinch's house, isn't it? You live there?"

"Yes. My mother's his housekeeper. Do you know Professor Bullfinch?"

"I guess everybody in Midston knows

about the Professor. So that's why you're so keen on science, eh? Well, so long. Stay out of trouble."

With a wave of his hand, Mr. Ellison crossed the street and got into a car parked there. The young people watched him drive off. The car was not a small one, but it looked small with him in it.

"Gosh, what a nice guy," Joe said. "I didn't know detectives were like that."

"Maybe all of them aren't," said Irene. "I wonder if he'll ever get in touch with us again, Danny?"

Danny didn't answer. He was staring into space with an absent-minded expression.

"Dan!" Irene poked him sharply.

"Huh? Oh, sorry. I was just thinking about being a detective."

He put the radiometer into the wagon and began towing it along, up Beckforth Street, toward home.

"You mean you've given up wanting to be a physicist?" said Joe, falling into step alongside him.

"Of course not. I was thinking that being

26

a detective must be something like being a scientist."

Irene stared at him. "What? I don't get that."

"Well, they both use a way of reasoning things out, don't they? Figuring out how a crime was done and who did it must be something like using the scientific method."

"What's the scientific method?" Joe asked.

"First, you set up a hypothesis—that is, a theory about why or how something works the way it does. Then you set up experiments which will either prove your idea or show that it's wrong. You might have some clues— for instance, an apple falling off a tree gave Newton a clue that helped him work out his theory about gravity."

Irene nodded. "That's right. And scientists collect evidence for a theory the way detectives collect it for a crime. I guess in some ways they are a lot alike."

"Well, okay," said Joe, who had been trudging along, listening, with his hands in his pockets. "Then you can use your scientific detective method to tell me why that man is acting the way he is."

He pointed ahead with a thrust of his chin. The man he indicated was pacing back and forth on the sidewalk in front of Professor Bullfinch's house, with his hands behind his back and his head bent. He was well dressed in a lightweight business suit, and wore a light gray hat. He had a neat pointed beard which made him look very distinguished. And yet there was something odd, even a little menacing about him. It came, Danny decided, from the thick-rimmed dark glasses which covered his eyes.

His behavior was certainly curious. He took three or four steps in one direction, stopped, gestured with one hand as if he were talking to himself, then turned and went three or four steps the other way. As the three friends stared, he shrugged and walked briskly up to the door of the Professor's house, raised his hand to ring the bell, dropped it, and returned to his pacing and gesturing on the sidewalk.

"I wonder who he is," Danny said. "He

looks as if he's having trouble making up his mind."

"Maybe he's an insurance salesman," said Joe. "And he isn't sure your mother needs any."

"He's no salesman. He's not carrying any briefcase or sample case," Danny objected. "I'll bet he wants to talk to Professor Bullfinch, but isn't sure whether the Professor wants to see him or not."

"Whoever he is, I don't like him," Irene said firmly. "There's something shifty about him."

"Maybe he's a secret agent," Joe hissed dramatically.

The bearded man suddenly made up his mind. He strode up the walk. But instead of going to the front door, he disappeared around the far side of the house.

"He's going to the Professor's laboratory," said Danny. "Come on, let's see what he's up to."

Professor Bullfinch's laboratory was a long, low extension built on the back of the house and facing the garden. Danny galloped along the sidewalk, the radiometer bumping and banging in the wagon. He cut across the lawn, and with the others at his heels, ran to the garden. He dropped the handle of the wagon. There was no trace of the bearded man.

30

"He must have gone inside," panted Irene.

Danny put a finger to his lips. Softly, he led the way to the rear door, which opened into the laboratory. It had four glass panes in the upper panel. The three friends crowded close, peering through the glass.

Inside, the bearded man and Professor Bullfinch stood facing each other across a stone-topped laboratory bench. And the Professor was pointing a pistol at the intruder.

THREE

An Unusual Request

Alarm bells rang in Danny's head. His only thought was to help the Professor—somehow, any way—although he had no clear idea how. Very often, Dan had been criticized for acting without careful thought, and now was no exception. Impulsively, he put his hand on the doorknob.

He had forgotten, however, that his friends were leaning on him, one at each shoulder, to look into the lab. The moment the knob turned, the door swung inward and all three children fell sprawling on their faces on the floor.

The noise startled the Professor. His hand jerked on the trigger. Danny, looking up, was just in time to see him fire the pistol.

What came out was not a bullet, but a huge blob of white foam. It spilled over the top of the lab bench, and part of it spattered over the front of the bearded man's jacket like great dollops of soapsuds from a washing machine.

"Hey!" cried the stranger, starting back.

"Great heavens!" exclaimed Professor Bullfinch. "Danny! That's no way to come into a room."

Dan scrambled to his feet. He stared at the Professor in confusion, and stammered, "I didn't mean—we thought he—I thought you—"

"Calm down." Professor Bullfinch's round face had resumed its usual cheery expression, and his eyes twinkled behind his spectacles. "You can explain in a moment. But first—"

The bearded man was examining with

horror the glops of foam on his jacket. "You've ruined my coat," he was saying.

"Not at all, my dear sir," said the Professor. "Just hold still." He bent forward, took hold of a corner of one of the blobs, and peeled it off the cloth with one firm movement. It came away in one piece leaving no mark behind.

"It has hardened, you see," he explained, tossing it on the lab bench. Quickly, he removed the others.

"Thank goodness for that," said the stranger. "This is a new suit. What is that stuff?"

"It's a liquid polymer," said the Professor, "which releases a gas that inflates it into foam when it comes out of this gun. When it's exposed to the air, it hardens into this spongy material. I was packing some delicate equipment to be sent to my friend, Dr. Grimes, in Washington, and I use the stuff to cushion it."

He motioned to a pair of wooden boxes on the bench. One of them contained a small, intricate machine, partly covered with the white material. "The foam protects the equipment and can be peeled away afterward without harming it, as you see. Now, Danny, perhaps you'll tell me why you and your friends came flying in that way. It's more usual to knock."

"Gee, we're sorry, Professor," Danny said shamefacedly. He glanced at Joe and Irene, who were tongue-tied. Joe made a helpless face; Irene sighed and shook her head. "The fact is—well, we saw this man out in front of the house acting very suspiciously, and we thought he might be a —" Looking at the stranger in his dapper spring suit, he suddenly realized how foolish his suspicions must sound, and finished in a mumble, "—a crook. It was the dark glasses that made him look that way, I guess."

Then he took a second look at the man. The frames were the same, but the lenses were ordinary clear glass. "But you aren't wearing dark glasses," he said, in astonishment. "I must be crazy."

The stranger smiled. "No, sonny, you're not. These are made of a specially treated glass which darkens in sunlight and clears up indoors. My eyes are sensitive, and this way I don't have to keep changing my glasses."

Now that they could see his eyes, he seemed like an ordinary, respectable businessman. The atmosphere cleared, and everyone began smiling with him.

"That's better," said the Professor. He laid aside his foam gun and perched himself on a high stool, motioning the stranger to another. "Make yourself comfortable," he said. He pulled out his pipe and began to fill it. In his old tweeds he looked very shabby alongside the smartly dressed stranger, and yet, he had an air of self-assurance and strength which made him stand out, whomever he was with. When you looked at him, Danny thought with admiration, you couldn't help saying, "Here's a *real* person!"

The Professor got his pipe going and then said to his visitor, "You hadn't gotten as far as introducing yourself before the youngsters—er—dropped in."

"My name is Anguish," the other man said. "Stanley Francis Anguish."

"Glad to know you. What can I do for you?"

Mr. Anguish looked meaningly at the three children, who were standing silently in a row. "It's confidential," he said.

"Come, come," said the Professor. "Don't you know that the more you try to hide something these days, the more people try to find it? The best way to keep something secret is to say it out loud, then nobody will believe you."

"Yes, hum, that's all very well," said Mr. Anguish, "but this is important. I want you to invent something for me, and I don't think these kiddies can be of any help."

"We're not—" Danny began, but a glance from the Professor silenced him.

"You might be surprised," the Professor said to Mr. Anguish. "If it will make you happy, I'll tell them to leave. But I assure you, they are trustworthy, and what's more, they often come up with excellent suggestions."

"Well, all right." Mr. Anguish stroked his beard, still looking as if he were not altogether convinced. "I want you to invent an uncrackable safe."

"A *what*?" exclaimed the Professor.

"Let me explain. I am the manager of Frognall & Pounder's."

"The Frog Pond?" The Professor smiled.

Frognall & Pounder's was the biggest department store in Midston, as well as the oldest. It took up a whole city block and for as long as anyone could remember, had been affectionately called The Frog Pond by everyone in town.

"As you may know," Mr. Anguish continued, "there has been an increase in crime recently. Frognall & Pounder's present store was put up in 1901, and while it is very attractive and convenient, it is somewhat old-fashioned. A great deal of money comes in, as you might imagine, and I've been worried that sooner or later it will attract a burglar. I've only been there for a year, and I am concerned that nothing should happen.

"On Saturdays, we stay open until five, which means that the day's takings are kept

in our safe until Monday. Also, we sometimes have special sales, which means that
the store stays open until very late. Old Mr.
Frognall never wanted to make any changes,
and so we have the same safe that was installed at the beginning of the century. It's
an antique. Now, however, the present
owner, Mr. Frognall's nephew, Mr. Chambers, has given me permission to have a new
safe put in. I want something foolproof, something no criminal will be able to open. I
thought you might help me."

"Dear me," said the Professor. "You
want a magician, not a scientist."

"I see. Then you can't do anything?" Mr.
Anguish picked up his hat.

"I didn't say that." The Professor looked
pensively into the bowl of his pipe. "However, you must know that no safe is absolutely
foolproof. It's hard to guard against a determined man with a few sticks of dynamite, for
instance."

"That's true. But our safe is on the top
floor of the building. Anyone who wanted to
blast it open would have to run the risk of
making all that noise and then escaping down

five floors, past our security guards. We take up a whole block, you know, so there's no other building next to us."

The Professor rested his chin on his hand and blew out a slow plume of smoke. He pondered in silence for a moment or two, and then said, "A good combination—"

"Combinations can be worked out with modern electronic equipment," said Mr. Anguish.

"A tumbler lock?"

"Locks can be picked."

"Special keys?"

"Keys can be duplicated."

"An electrically operated bolt?"

"Electric wires can be cut."

The Professor hummed. "Quite a problem."

Then Danny said, almost to himself, "Maybe the best thing would be a good watchdog, trained to sniff out strangers."

"Watchdogs can be poisoned," droned Mr. Anguish, in the same tone he had used before.

"Not if they're robots," Danny said.

The Professor snapped erect. He took the pipe out of his mouth and pointed the stem at Danny.

"Why not?" Danny went on. "It wouldn't be hard to build a little machine powered by batteries that would roll it around. You'd have a heat-seeking cell in its head so it could go after any person who broke in—"

"It could have a pair of claws so it could grab anyone it was chasing," Irene said.

"Sure," said Danny. He thought for a moment. "The only real trouble is, how could it tell a crook from anybody else?" He shook his head. "It might end up grabbing a guard while the safecracker escaped. Oh, well, forget it."

"Not at all," said the Professor. "You've given me an idea."

Mr. Anguish had been staring in amazement from one to the other. Now he put in, "Surely, you aren't serious? Robot watchdogs? How on earth would we manage them? We'd have to have an engineer on duty! How could a machine tell a burglar from a guard? How—?"

"Be calm, Mr. Anguish," said the Professor mildly. "You're quite right, a robot watchdog isn't the answer to your problem. But perhaps we could make a lock that would be able to sniff out friend from foe."

"You mean," Mr. Anguish said uncertainly, "it would need some sort of identification—a picture, perhaps—?"

"I mean *sniff*," the Professor replied. "Just as a dog does."

"But—" Mr. Anguish began.

Professor Bullfinch jumped down from his stool. The laboratory was a long, cluttered room, its center taken up by two stone-topped benches littered with bunsen burners, glassware, and electronic equipment, its walls lined with shelves loaded with more materials for his experiments. In one corner, where the light from one of the big windows fell on it, was a blackboard. The Professor made his way to it, picked up a piece of chalk, and beckoned the others to join him. Mr. Anguish watched with his hands behind his back. Dan perched himself on the nearest bench, Irene leaned against the windowsill, and Joe, sitting on a stool, fished the remains of a very dusty chocolate bar out of his pocket and began peeling the paper from it.

"Don't mind me," he said. "I won't understand any of this anyway."

The Professor said, "I will now draw you a picture of a smell."

Quickly, he chalked a diagram on the board:

$$H \diagdown_{S} \diagup H$$

Irene cocked her head on one side. "Two hydrogen atoms and a sulphur atom. Oh, I know—a molecule of hydrogen sulfide."

"Exactly," said the Professor. "The smell of a rotten egg." He put down the chalk and dusted his hands. "Smells are molecules evaporating off the surfaces of various substances and carried by air currents. It is the structure and shape and chemical formulae of these molecules which make a smell."

"You see?" Joe said, biting into his chocolate in a satisfied way. "I told you I wouldn't understand."

The Professor chuckled. "I won't go into

any more details, then," he said. "The point is, your warm skin is continually releasing molecules into the air, and these are formed into patterns that are distinctive to your own body chemistry. We don't know exactly how a dog can recognize its master's smell because not enough is known yet about the exact way in which the molecules are received by the nerve cells, or even what it is precisely which makes these molecules recognized as smells. But in theory, it ought to be possible to make a machine which would sort out and recognize the pattern of molecules given off by a particular person."

"Smell-o-vision," said Joe.

The Professor laughed. "More like Danny's robot watchdog. In practice, it would be a lock which sniffed at Mr. Anguish's hand, recognized his scent, and opened for him and for him alone."

"That's the answer!" Mr. Anguish said. "By George, do you really think it can be done?"

Professor Bullfinch cupped his chin in his hand. "Give me a few weeks," he said in an abstracted tone, "and I'll tell you."

FOUR

"Fee Fi Fo Fum!"

Summer was nearly over. It had been long and happy for Danny and his friends, full of picnics and hiking trips, fishing and games, and lazy loafing in the sun with a good book. Dan and his mother had made a three-week expedition to Colorado, where Mrs. Dunn had a cousin in Boulder, and they had driven to the Rocky Mountain National Park for a week of camping. All that time, since the day in spring when Mr. Anguish had asked for help, Professor Bullfinch had been deeply

47

immersed in the problem; at first in his laboratory, then in consultation with engineers, and then overseeing the making and installation of the new safe.

Toward the end of August, one morning at breakfast, he said to Danny, "Today's the day."

Dan was not yet completely awake. Spearing a piece of bacon, he said with a yawn, "What day? It's Thursday, isn't it?"

"Come, come, Dan, you're not thinking. We're going to The Frog Pond for the final tests of the safe."

Danny's eyes snapped wide open. "I forgot. When are we going? Shall I call Joe and Irene now?"

"We're due there at ten. Are you coming with us, Mrs. Dunn?"

Mrs. Dunn shook her head. "I don't think so. I have too much to do this morning. You can tell me about it at lunch."

Danny gobbled the rest of his breakfast and phoned his friends. Soon after, Irene came over, wearing a white sleeveless blouse and a short blue skirt instead of her usual blue jeans. "It felt like a dress-uppy sort of occasion," she explained.

They waited at the door to the laboratory, fidgeting impatiently until the Professor told them to stop dangling about like a pair of earrings. Joe joined them shortly, munching a piece of toast which, he said, he had found doing nothing in the kitchen as he came in. "I felt sorry for it—it looked so lonely," he told them.

The Professor was ready at last. He came out of the lab, cramming his hat on with one hand and carrying a small metal case in the other. "Let's go," he said. "We've plenty of time, so perhaps you won't mind walking. I need to stretch my legs." He pointed to the sun. "What on earth is that bright yellow thing up there? I've been working indoors so long, I've forgotten what the outside world looks like."

It was only a half hour's walk to the bustling business section of Midston. On the way, Joe said, "I've written a poem in honor of the new safe. Would you like to hear it?"

"Certainly," said Professor Bullfinch.

Joe cleared his throat, and recited:

"We are lost," the captain shouted,
As he staggered down the deck,
"There's a burglar close behind me
And he's breathing down my neck."
"Never mind," the first mate answered,
"Put your money in this box.
It is made of iron, and it has
The Bullfinch special locks."
"Don't be silly," cried the burglar,
And he bowed and raised his hat.
"I don't want your gold and silver,
All I want's a safe like that."

"Very—" began the Professor, but Joe raised his hand.

"There's more," he said, "The final couplet."

Poems are made by this sad waif,
But only the Prof. can make a safe.

He bowed smugly. Professor Bullfinch began laughing. "Very fine and very flattering," he said.

"How does he do it?" Irene said, with admiration.

"The same way you work out math problems in your head," said Danny.

Frognall & Pounder's store was an imposing square block of dark-brown stone. It had been built at a time when dignity required decoration, and around the windows of the upper stories crept foliage and flowers cut in stone, while over its big front doors was a carving of the Goddess of Business pouring riches out of a cornucopia into the hands of grateful customers. Inside, it had high ceilings in which old-fashioned electric fans were still set, although air conditioning had also been installed as a gesture to the modern world. The walls were marble; the elevators had polished brass doors.

The Professor looked around with satisfaction. "They don't make stores like this anymore," he said. "It's a pleasure to shop in a place like this."

They took the elevator to the top floor, and found themselves among beds and mattresses, dining-room tables, and vast over-

stuffed armchairs. A floorwalker in a dark suit, who spoke in hushed, solemn tones as if he were in church, showed them the way to the office. Two security guards stood outside. One opened the door and called out an elderly secretary, who led the Professor and the three young people inside.

"Good morning, Professor," said Mr. Anguish, coming from behind his desk to greet them. "I see you have your—hm—young assistants with you. And how are we this morning, kiddies?"

"If he pats me on the head," Joe whispered in Irene's ear, "I'll bite him."

Mr. Anguish didn't hear, for he was paying no further attention to the children. He motioned to a thin, bitter-looking man who was waiting in a corner of the office.

He said to the Professor, "You already know my assistant manager, Mr. String."

"Yes, of course. Good morning."

Mr. String bobbed his head curtly. He had an angry, wrinkled face and his mouth looked as if he had just found salt instead of sugar in his coffee. "We'd better get on with this nonsense," he said, in a voice to match the rest of him. "It's getting late, Mr. Anguish, and there's a lot of work piling up."

"I am perfectly well aware of it, Mr. String," Mr. Anguish replied. And to the

Professor, he added, "Mr. String doesn't approve of the new safe. He thinks old Mr. Frognall wouldn't have liked it."

"Certainly not," Mr. String said. "Thirty-seven years I've been with this store, and we did all right without this new-fangled fiddle-faddle. Air conditioning. Computers. And now locks that smell people. Rubbish!"

"All right," Mr. Anguish said coldly. "That's enough. Let's begin, Professor."

He did not see the look of hatred Mr. String gave him, but Danny did. "They sure don't like each other," he thought. "And I don't think I care much for Mr. String, either. I wouldn't trust him if I were Mr. Anguish."

Professor Bullfinch put the small case he had brought with him on the desk, and then walked over to examine the new safe that had been built into one wall of the office. Its gray steel door, more than two feet thick, stood open. The old safe, a large black affair decorated with gold bands, had been moved into a corner where it took up far too much room. As soon as its contents had been transferred to the new one, it would be taken away.

The Professor finished his inspection and returned to the desk. He opened the metal case and from it carefully took two strips of silvery paper covered with fine dark lines.

"These," he explained, "are your identification tapes. This is yours, Mr. Anguish, and the other is Mr. String's. As you know, in

each case, we have already analyzed the pattern of molecules given off as a distinctive odor from your skin, and those patterns have been imprinted on the tapes."

He went to the safe and opened a panel on the inside of the heavy door. He inserted the tapes in a receptacle and closed the panel. Then he swung the door shut. There was a faint double click.

"Locked," he said. "Closing the door automatically shoots the double steel bolts. As you know, Mr. Anguish, I have embedded a battery inside the door itself. So there are no wires that can be cut to shut off the power. The battery controls an electromagnet which will draw the bolts. But of course, it will only operate when the right key is put into the lock."

"A key?" Danny interrupted. "I didn't know there was a key."

"I'm only joking," said the Professor. "The key is either Mr. Anguish's hand or Mr. String's."

In the front of the steel door was a slot, about two inches by five inches. The Professor tapped it with a stubby finger.

"Inside this," he said, "is our watchdog, to use Danny's word. Without getting too complicated, I can say that it's a sort of gelatine membrane covered with hundreds of tiny ion-selective electrodes. In the gel are chemicals which react with the molecules of scent coming from your hand and make ions—that is, bits of molecules—which are then filtered through the membrane. They are received by the electrodes and generate a tiny signal. The signals are identified by a mini-computer, and when the right pattern of signals is received, matching the patterns on the tapes, the lock will open."

"We hope it will open," said Mr. String sourly. "In my experience, something always goes wrong with this modern gadgetry."

"The only thing that can go wrong, I believe, is for the battery to run down," said the Professor gently. "I forgot to mention that there is a cable running to it from the building's power source. Once a week it will be automatically recharged, if it needs it. But I don't think—"

He paused, for there was the sound of loud voices outside the office door. "Is something wrong out there?" he asked.

Mr. Anguish strode to the door and threw it open. "What's going on?" he demanded.

Through the open door, they could all see that the two security guards were holding a young man between them. He had shaggy hair down to his shoulders, and a shaggy beard. His old army jacket was torn and the ends of his jeans were ragged.

"We caught this character snooping

around out here," said one of the guards. "He says he wants to see you."

"Me?" said Mr. Anguish. "All right, let him go."

He stepped outside the office and beckoned to the young man, who dusted off his sleeves with a haughty glance at the guards and joined him. The pair stood just out of earshot, talking in low voices for a moment, and then the young man pulled something out of his pocket and showed it to the manager, who nodded.

"Oh, very well, very well," he said irritably. "Come back in half an hour. I'll settle it then."

The young man went off, and Mr. Anguish returned to the office.

"What was all that?" asked Mr. String.

"Nothing important. Let's continue, shall we, Professor?"

"Right," said Professor Bullfinch. "I think everything's ready for a trial. First, we'll try a couple of the wrong hands. Dan, suppose you put your right hand into the slot."

Danny marched forward and thrust his hand into the opening on the door of the safe. He felt a gentle warmth, but nothing happened.

"Good," said the Professor. "Now, Irene, and then Joe."

When they had done so, he nodded to Mr. Anguish. "Now, you try. Put your hand in, leave it there for a count of three, and remove it."

"He's going to have his palm read," Joe remarked.

Irene giggled.

The manager put his hand into the slot. They heard once again the soft *click-click*. The heavy door swung open.

"You know what it said, don't you?" said the irrepressible Joe. "'Fee, fi, fo, fum! I smell the blood of a department store manager.'"

The Professor chuckled, and even Mr. String gave a tiny, acid smile.

"Now, Mr. String, it's your turn," said the Professor, pushing the door shut again.

The door opened obediently to the assistant manager's hand.

"Excellent!" said Mr. Anguish. "I congratulate you, Professor."

"Thank you," Professor Bullfinch said. "But properly, you should be grateful to Danny. After all, he gave me the original idea."

Mr. Anguish nodded. Then he went to his desk and wrote something on a piece of paper.

"Here, my boy," he said, holding it out to Dan. "Take this. This store has a fine, old-fashioned soda fountain on the ground floor. I'm sure you and your two friends can find your way to it."

The note said, *Please give my guests anything they want. S. F. Anguish, Manager.*

"Now this," said Joe, as a short time later they settled themselves around a marble-topped table in front of three enormous chocolate sundaes piled high with whipped cream, "is what I call being *really* grateful."

FIVE

A Disappearance

Draped over a kitchen chair, Danny watched his mother deftly preparing vegetables for a lovely French stew called a *daube*. With a large triangular knife, she chopped carrots into neat disks and set them aside, and then began slicing onions.

"For heaven's sake, Danny," she said, wiping away an oniony tear with the back of one hand, "go away. Do something. What's the matter with you?"

62

"In nine days, and thirteen and a half hours, school starts," Danny replied.

"Good figuring. How many minutes?" Mrs. Dunn dried the blade of her knife and turned to the tomatoes.

"And the Professor's gone away. That makes it sort of forlorn," Danny said. "There's always something to do or talk about when he's around."

"Heavens, Dan! He only left yesterday morning. Where's Joe?"

"Went to get a haircut," Danny mumbled.

"Irene?"

"Playing tennis with Heather Glenn."

"Well—where's the garlic? Ah, hiding under that onion skin. Well, why don't you—oh, I don't know—go into the lab and invent something? Whatever you do, get out from underfoot."

Danny gave a long sigh and very slowly began to untangle himself from the chair. Just then there was a loud knock at the kitchen door.

"See who it is, dear," said Mrs. Dunn.

Danny pulled the door open. A familiar

black face looked down at him with a flash of white teeth.

"Mr. Ellison!" said Danny. "Hi!"

"Hello, Dan. Found any ghosts yet?" asked the detective.

Mrs. Dunn stared at her son and then at the visitor in surprise.

"This is Mr. Ellison, Mom," Danny said.

The detective showed Mrs. Dunn his badge.

"How do you do?" said Mrs. Dunn. "Excuse me if I seem a trifle confused. What's all this about ghosts? I thought the police department was interested in catching live people."

"In general, we are. However, I met your son when he was trying an experiment in ghost-finding."

"I'll believe anything where Danny is concerned," said Mrs. Dunn. "Please come in. Would you like a cup of coffee?"

"Thank you." Mr. Ellison took the chair Danny pulled out for him. "By the way, Dan, that was a good deduction you made. Do you remember it?"

"You mean, about the lights in the house?"

"That's right. You see, Mrs. Dunn, when I first met Dan I was investigating the appearance of lights in an old, deserted house on Beckforth Street."

"I think I know the one. But what was Danny doing there?"

Dan quickly explained how he and his friends had tried using the radiometer to locate ghosts.

Mr. Ellison then went on, "Danny suggested that someone might have been looking around with an oil lamp and that it went out. Well, back in July we arrested an old tramp who had broken into a hunting lodge. He confessed that he had also gone into the house on Beckforth Street one chilly evening. He had found a rusty oil lamp and some kerosene in the pantry. He had filled the lamp and taken it upstairs because, if you remember, there was a cot in the middle bedroom. He put the lamp on the floor, but it was old and leaky, and the kerosene ran out all over the floor. When he left, he took the lamp with him, figuring he could sell it for a few cents."

"Gee, then I really was pretty close," said Danny. "Maybe the scientific method would work for a detective."

"The scientific method?"

"It's a way of finding out whether something is true or not by logic and experiment," Danny said. "I think it must be something like what you do when you're trying to work out who committed a crime."

"I guess so," Mr. Ellison said, a bit doubtfully. "And speaking of science—um—brings me to why I'm here."

He sipped his coffee. "This is very good," he said. "It tastes like fresh-ground Blue Mountain, from Jamaica."

"Right the first time," said Mrs. Dunn, looking pleased. "I buy the beans and grind them myself. You're a coffee expert, all right."

"Not really, but I do like my food and drink." He took another mouthful, put down the cup, and went on, "Can you tell me where Professor Bullfinch is?"

"Why, yes. He's in Washington, attend-

ing some sort of conference," said Mrs. Dunn. "He left yesterday."

Mr. Ellison nodded. "We know that. He took the ten o'clock plane. We've checked. What I want is his address there. Did he leave you one?"

Mrs. Dunn had a little desk in one corner of the kitchen. Above it were shelves full of cookbooks, and below it she kept her records, bills, and other papers. She got from it a slip of paper.

"He's staying at the Berkeley Hotel. It's small and cheap, and a good many scientists go there. Here's the address."

Mr. Ellison copied it down in a notebook. "Many thanks."

"What's this about?" Danny asked. "Why do you want the Professor? Do you need his advice about something?"

"Not exactly. We just want to have a word with him."

Mrs. Dunn's face took on an expression Danny knew well. It was her *I know you're not telling me the whole truth* expression.

"Mr. Ellison," she said crisply. "I think you're hiding something. I know it's our duty to help the police, but I think you owe it to us to tell us what's going on. Is Professor Bullfinch in some kind of trouble?"

The big detective shifted uneasily under her gaze. He looked at Danny, and the boy grinned sympathetically at him, knowing just how uncomfortable that tone of Mrs. Dunn's could make you feel.

"Well, the fact is," Mr. Ellison said at last, "we want to talk to him in connection with a disappearance."

"A disappearance?" Danny and his mother spoke together.

"A man has vanished," the detective went on, "and as far as we know, Professor Bullfinch is the last person to have spoken to him."

"What man?" said Danny. "Who is he?"

"His name is Stanley Anguish. He is the manager of—"

"The Frog Pond," Danny finished. "Where has he gone?"

"That's what we're trying to find out," said Mr. Ellison. "So far, we haven't a lead. You know Mr. Anguish, do you?"

"I've met him," Danny admitted. "Professor Bullfinch made a new kind of safe for the store."

"So I've heard. Well, Mr. Anguish is a man of regular habits. He left his house every morning at eight-thirty and walked to the store, following exactly the same route and arriving at nine. He had his lunch at exactly twelve, always in the store restaurant, and returned to work at twelve forty-five. Except when there were special sales and the store stayed open late, he left at six and walked home. He followed this routine every day, rain or shine." Mr. Ellison paused. "Except yesterday," he added.

"What happened then?" said Mrs. Dunn.

"He left the house as usual, according to the neighbors, but he never arrived at the store. At nine-thirty, the assistant manager, Mr. String, telephoned his house. Mr. Anguish has a housekeeper who does his cleaning and cooking, but Mr. String knew that she had gone on vacation a few days before. However, he thought Mr. Anguish might be sick. There was no answer to his call, so he opened the store at ten, and when Mr. Anguish still hadn't turned up at eleven, he called the police.

"We have established that Mr. Anguish did not return after leaving the house. He took his usual walk and went into a little shop at the corner of Main Street and Glenn Road at a quarter to nine, just as he did every morning, to buy some cigars. When he left the shop, the owner happened to glance after him through the window and saw a taxi stop at the curb. He saw Mr. Anguish talk to someone in the cab. He says he is certain it was Professor Bullfinch. He recognized him because the Professor sometimes comes in to buy tobacco. The cab drove away, and Mr. Anguish kept on walking. From that spot, it usually only took him about ten minutes more to get to Frognall & Pounder's, but during that ten minutes he seems to have vanished completely, and no one has seen him since."

Mr. Ellison regarded them gravely. They stared back at him, Mrs. Dunn frowning, Danny gaping.

Mrs. Dunn said, "Surely, Mr. Ellison, whatever has happened to that man, you don't suspect that the Professor had anything to do with it?"

The detective shook his head. "I don't suspect anything, Mrs. Dunn. My job right now is simply to gather some facts, and try to get a lead on what happened. My chief, Detective Sergeant Macedo, is the one who feels the Professor may know something."

He rose to his feet and took up his hat. "I'm sorry to have disturbed you. However, if you should think of anything you can tell me in connection with this case, please get in touch with me at Police Headquarters. I'll leave you the phone number and extension."

He wrote it down on a page which he tore from his notebook, and put it on the table. To Dan, he added, "I still haven't come across any good hauntings, but if I do, I won't forget you."

"Thanks," Danny said automatically. His mind, however, was on other things.

When the detective had gone, Danny said, "I don't know what's happened to Mr. Anguish, Mom, but I'll bet Professor Bullfinch didn't have anything to do with it. I *know* he didn't."

"I'm sure you're right," said his mother. "But we can't prove it."

"Yes, we can. We can phone him."

"Phone the Professor?" She glanced at

the kitchen clock. "It's past ten. Surely, he won't be at the hotel now. He must have gone to his meeting."

"Yes, but you can phone the hotel and leave a message for him. Maybe he'll check in there during the day. Tell him to call home. Go ahead, Mom, please!" Danny said urgently. "I know what happened. He was on his way to the airport and saw Mr. Anguish on the street, and just stopped the cab long enough to ask him how the new safe was working out. I'm sure that's all it was. But let's not wait—let's find out as soon as we can."

"All right," said Mrs. Dunn, who was as anxious as Danny to know what had happened.

She dialed the number of the hotel in Washington, while Dan nervously nibbled the skin at the corner of one of his fingernails. He could hear the hum as the number rang.

Then his mother said, "Professor Euclid Bullfinch, please."

She waited, and Dan could hear the tinny little telephone voice saying something.

"What?" said his mother. "I don't understand. Are you sure?"

She hung up, and turned to face Dan with an expression in which alarm and bewilderment were mingled.

"What did they say?" Danny asked.

"They have no such person registered there," said Mrs. Dunn.

SIX

"It Could Be a Clue!"

"What are you going to do now?" Joe asked.

He had come to Danny's house after getting his hair cut, and with the talent for which he was famous had arrived at the precise moment when Mrs. Dunn put a plate of chocolate brownies on the table. It was a few minutes after the phone call to Washington, and Mrs. Dunn had said that both she and Dan needed something to give them strength. They had told Joe about Mr. Ellison's visit and their discovery that the Professor was not registered in his hotel.

"There isn't anything we *can* do," Danny said. "There's no point in our calling the police because they will know as much as we do as soon as Mr. Ellison phones that number."

"I'm not really worried," Mrs. Dunn said. "I know there's some explanation, and we'll learn it in due time. But I can't help being worried—"

She stopped, and couldn't keep from grinning. "I'm also mixed up," she said.

Danny got up, his mouth full of cake, and put his arm around his mother's neck. "Don't worry, Mom," he said, kissing her and leaving a sprinkling of chocolate crumbs on her cheek. "I'm sure everything will work out."

Mrs. Dunn smiled at him, brushing herself off. "Okay. You're very comforting in a crumbly sort of way. I'll get back to work."

"Come on, Joe," Danny said. "Let's go play some baseball."

Joe took another brownie. "Thanks, Mrs. Dunn," he said. "Dan's right. Don't worry. The police will handle everything."

The boys went outside, and Dan led the way to a big clump of lilacs between his house and Irene's, one of his favorite spots for thinking and planning.

"All right," Joe said. "Now what's all this baseball stuff? You know I'm no good at the game. You obviously have something else in your head."

"Yes, I have," Dan said, seating himself on the ground under the thick tent of green leaves. "It's this. There isn't anything we can do to find the Professor—not unless we could get to Washington, and we can't do that. But maybe we can find Mr. Anguish. After all, he disappeared right here in Midston."

Joe sniffed soberly at his last brownie. "That ought to be about as easy as finding a four-leaf clover in January. And correct me if I'm wrong, but aren't the cops trying to find him, too?"

"Sure. But so far they haven't had any luck. We can't do any worse, can we? And we'll use the scientific method."

"Oh, yeah, I remember that. You know something?"

"What?"

"We're going to get into trouble."

"Oh, don't be such a glomp!"

"Hm? What's a glomp?" Joe said, looking interested.

"I don't know, but don't be one. Now, listen. The first step is to gather some facts so we can set up a hypothesis—a theory, you know—about what happened."

Joe stuffed the rest of the brownie into his mouth. "Oogah. Hargh hum—" He swallowed hastily, and started over. "Okay. Fact one. Mr. Anguish walked out of his house the way he does every day, walked down the street, said something to Professor Bullfinch, and vanished."

"What could he have said, I wonder?" Danny mused.

"Good-bye?" suggested Joe.

Danny rolled up his eyes.

"No, but seriously," Joe said, "do you think there was any real connection? Do you think the Professor had anything to do with Mr. Anguish's disappearance?"

"No, I don't. I think the cops may try to

make it look that way, but the Professor was on his way to the airport, and he did take his plane. I'm sure he just stopped to chat for a minute."

"How do we know he really took the plane?"

"Because Mr. Ellison said the police had checked up on it. No, Joe, we haven't got any facts, yet. I think one of the best ways to find out where somebody's gone is to start from where he started and follow his tracks. Let's go to Mr. Anguish's house and start from there."

"What about Irene? Aren't you going to wait for her?"

Danny struggled for a moment inside himself. He wanted to get started at once, but his loyalty to his friends was stronger. "Yes," he said, at last. "She'll be finished with tennis by noon. And three heads are better than two."

"Especially when one of them's mine," Joe said cheerfully. "I'm glad you decided that way."

"Yes, well, we can't leave Irene out."

"Oh, I wasn't thinking of that. But it's only half an hour to lunch, and I detect better on a full stomach."

Right after lunch, the three friends met at Joe's house. On the way there, Danny had told Irene everything. She was as eager as he to learn the truth.

"But I think," she said, "maybe we ought to ask around the neighborhood and see if anyone noticed anything when Mr. Anguish left his house. Maybe someone followed him—"

"Good idea," said Danny. "But we can't just ask people if they saw any suspicious characters. They'll say, 'What business is it of a bunch of kids?'"

"It depends on how you ask," Irene said. "Let me try. I can look more innocent than either of you boys."

Before they left Joe's house, she asked Mrs. Pearson for an envelope.

"What's that for?" asked Danny.

"It's a way of starting a conversation," Irene said primly. "You'll see."

They got Mr. Anguish's address from the phone book. It was a longish walk, but the day was clear and cool, and they didn't mind. The street where Mr. Anguish lived was near a small park on the edge of town, a neighborhood of one- and two-family houses, many of them rather shabby, with worn and peeling paint. Most of them were squeezed together, but they all had little backyards, separated by wooden fences, and along the cracked sidewalks were small, brave trees. Toys and bicycles lay on many of the grubby front lawns, and laundry flapped in the breeze behind the houses. It all looked run-down but cheerful.

"Somehow, it's not exactly the place where I thought the manager of the biggest department store in Midston would live," said Irene.

Mr. Anguish's house stood on a corner, a little apart from its nearest neighbor, as if it were keeping to itself. It had a front porch overgrown by ragged wisteria that looked as if it hadn't been much cared for. The windows were masked by lace-edged curtains. The three friends inspected it for a moment.

Then Danny boldly went up on the porch and, cupping his hands around his eyes, peered into one of the windows.

"See anybody?" Joe asked.

"Nope. I can't see anything. It's too dark."

He joined the others, and went on, "Now, what, Irene? You're in charge of this."

"Okay. Let me do the talking." She marched over to the next house and rang the bell.

A fat woman, whose hair looked like an abandoned bird's nest, opened the door and stared suspiciously at the three. "What do you want?" she said.

"Please excuse me," Irene said, with a winning smile, "but I have a note to deliver to Mr. Anguish, who lives next door." She held up the envelope she had taken from Mrs. Pearson. "I was told he'd be at home today. We knocked and rang, but there was no answer. Do you know when he's coming back?"

"I didn't know he was away," said the fat woman. "He's not much of a neighbor. He's lived next door for about a year, and never so

82

much as come over to say hello. The same with that snooty woman who keeps house for him. If they're both gone, good riddance to them."

"Oh. I'm sorry," Irene said. "Then you didn't see whether he left home yesterday or not, I suppose."

"I keep my nose out of other people's business," said the woman, and slammed the door.

"Whew! Mr. Anguish doesn't sound popular," Danny said. "I wonder if everybody feels that way about him?"

"We'll find out," said Irene, going on to the next house.

Fifteen minutes later, they had worked their way down the block. Some people were polite and friendly, one or two were grumpy, and in one house there was nobody but an old, old man who was playing a record of military marches at full volume and who only smiled and nodded at them, pointing to his ear. From most people, they heard the same story: Mr. Anguish had always kept pretty much to himself, had no friends in the neighborhood and few visitors. Some people had seen him going to work every day, or coming home in the evening, and those he met on the street he always said hello to in a pleasant enough way, but it never went any further.

"I don't think we're going to find out much about him," Danny said, running a hand through his red hair.

"It looks that way," said Irene. "Let's try one or two houses on the other street, and if that's no good we'll have to think of something else."

They went back to Mr. Anguish's house. Because of the corner, there was a bit more lawn to be shared with the first house on the adjoining street. That was a rather pretty place with trellis roses growing up its walls and a big porch that ran around two sides of it. On the porch, on a rocker, sat a gray little woman, knitting. Her hair, face, and dress were all the same shade of gray. As Irene and the boys approached, she smiled and nodded without stopping her rocking or the clicking of her needles.

Irene showed her the envelope and asked if she knew where Mr. Anguish was.

"Bless you, dearie," the woman said, in a

faint, gray sort of voice, "he's gone off somewhere. The police were here asking about
him only yesterday. He went off to work as
he always does, but he never did come back."

"Really?" said Irene. "Are you a friend
of his?"

"Oh, no, dearie. It's my belief he doesn't have any friends, poor soul. But I like to keep an eye on everything that goes on in the neighborhood, and I see him going and coming. Why, you could set your clock by him, most times. That's why I was so surprised when he never came home yesterday. Who did you say gave you the note?"

"Why—um—" said Irene, thinking fast. "A man stopped us on the street a while ago, and asked us to deliver it. I don't know who he was."

"That's funny. My goodness, that's funny, isn't it? Was he a ragged sort of man?"

"Ragged?" At the unexpected question, Irene's mind went blank. "I—I don't know. I mean, I don't know what you mean."

"Dressed in raggedy clothes, with a dirty old cap like a tramp."

"A tramp?" Irene stared. "Why? Have you seen somebody like that around here?"

"Oh, yes, indeedy, isn't that curious? Yesterday morning, soon after Mr. Anguish left his house. I was just looking out, as I always do, to see what's going on, because when you live all alone the way I do it's so interesting to watch life—don't you think so?"

"Yes, I do," said Irene. "You were going to tell me about that tramp."

"Of course, dearie. Well, he came walking around the corner and went up to Mr. Anguish's back door. I knew nobody was home, because Mrs. Botter, who works for him, went away last week and hasn't come back yet. I guess she must have gone on vacation. I thought I'd better keep an eye on him. He was drunk—you know how tramps are, dearie—and he was staggering and tripping, and he walked into the railing at the back-door steps and almost fell down. I got nervous—well, you know how it is—and I went to phone the police."

"Did they come?"

"Oh, yes, right away. But by then the tramp was gone." She looked at Irene out of pale, gray eyes, and said in her faint voice, "Don't you think I was right to call them anyway?"

"You certainly were," said Irene. "Did they look for the tramp?"

"Yes, they thought he might have tried

to break into Mr. Anguish's house, but the doors were all locked up tight. But then, when you said a man gave you that note—"

"Oh, no," Irene said quickly. "It wasn't any tramp. It was a well-dressed man. Maybe he was somebody who was in business with Mr. Anguish. Maybe he was a friend."

"Maybe he was. But I didn't know the poor soul had any friends. You learn something every day, don't you?"

"You certainly do," said Irene. "Good-bye, and thank you very much."

They left her rocking and knitting, and when they were around the corner and out of sight, Danny said, "You sure didn't have any trouble making *her* talk. And she was right. You learn something every day."

"What have we learned?" Joe asked. "Just that an old tramp came to Mr. Anguish's door for a handout, and when nobody answered, he took off again."

Danny turned to Irene. "Is that all you think, too?"

"Why, yes, Dan. What else?"

Danny shook his head at his friends. He looked so much like a teacher about to tell them to do their homework over again that Irene burst out laughing.

"Okay, laugh," he said. "But I've seen Mr. Anguish talking to a ragged man—and so have you."

"What? When was this?" Joe cried.

"Only a week or so ago, when we were in his office in the store. Remember? The day the Professor tested the watchdog lock."

"That's right," said Irene, snapping her fingers. "I do remember. But that was a young man, and this one was old."

"Was he?" Danny retorted. "That woman never said so. All she said was that he was dressed in raggedy clothes, with a dirty old cap, like a tramp. She never said whether he was young or old."

"But that young man looked more like a hippie than a tramp," Irene objected.

"Do you really think that woman would have known the difference?" Danny said.

"I guess not."

"It could be a clue," said Joe. "But if it is, it doesn't get us much further. How are we ever going to find that ragged guy again? This case is full of disappearances."

They walked on in silence for a time. At length, Irene said, with a sigh, "The whole thing really depends on those few minutes after Mr. Anguish left the tobacco shop. If only we had a bloodhound. Then we could start from Mr. Anguish's house and follow his trail."

"That's great," said Joe. "If only. Where could we get a bloodhound?"

Danny stopped short.

"What is it?" Irene said.

"A bloodhound!" Danny repeated. Then he gave a crow of laughter.

"He's gone crazy," said Joe. "Let's hold him down and call an ambulance."

Danny waved him away. "I know where we can get a bloodhound," he said. "We'll make one!"

SEVEN

Bleeper the Bloodhound

"Now I *know* he's gone crazy," said Joe. "I knew it would happen some day. The great brain has snapped."

"Oh, stop being silly, Joe," Irene said. "I think I know what he means. You've got some idea about using the Professor's watch-dog lock, haven't you, Dan? But how?"

"Come on back to my house," Danny said. "I'll show you."

They hurried along without more talk, and once back at Dan's house, he led them to the Professor's laboratory. One end of the long room was partitioned off to make an office in which were the Professor's desk, some filing cabinets, and a number of reference books and notebooks. From the top drawer of the desk, Dan took a flat box.

"Here you are," he said, lifting an envelope from it. "This contains a duplicate identification tape of Mr. Anguish's scent."

"I see," Irene said. "Now, if we had another watchdog—"

"Yep. The prototype of the device the Professor used in the safe is out in the lab," said Danny. "It's in separate parts, but I know how to hook it together. All we need is, first, some way to carry it."

"Let's look at it and see how big the parts are," Irene suggested.

Dan led his friends to one of the cabinets in which equipment was stored. Neatly ranged on shelves and covered with plastic sheeting were the panels of membrane containing the ion-selective electrodes, the miniature computer, and the battery and switches.

"All this stuff's been miniaturized," Danny said. "You can see that it doesn't take up much room."

"It wouldn't, would it? It had to go inside the door of the safe," said Irene. "Listen, out in my garage we've got an old vacuum cleaner that my mother doesn't use anymore. It's the kind with a tank you can carry around with one hand, and a long hose or nozzle with a kind of brush thing on the end of it. Why don't we pull the insides out of it and then we can mount the equipment in the tank?"

"Fine," said Danny. "And instead of a brush, we'll put the electrode panels at the end of the nozzle. Then we can carry the whole thing around like a metal detector."

"I don't understand how this is going to work," Joe complained. "It's just supposed to open a safe, isn't it? But Mr. Anguish wasn't carrying any safes around with him."

"All we want it to do is recognize his smell, just the way it does in the safe," said Danny. "Then we can follow his trail."

"Well, okay, if it could bark—" Joe began.

"It will." Danny snickered. "We've got a

Geiger counter here with a signal in it that goes 'bleep!' instead of clicking. I'll take the signal device out and hook it up to the wires of this thing. Then, when it recognizes the pattern of Mr. Anguish's scent, it'll bleep, and all we have to do is follow the bleeps."

In spite of Danny's optimistic prediction that the job wouldn't take long, he and Irene worked all the rest of the afternoon and half the next day. Joe recited poetry to them for a while to encourage them, as he said, but soon gave it up for they were too busy to listen. At last, however, they were done. Danny had been going outside every half hour or so to look anxiously at the sky, because clouds had been gathering and he felt that rain would wash away the traces of Mr. Anguish's trail. Even as it was, he admitted to Irene as they soldered the last connections, he wasn't really certain the device would work.

"Shall we try it right now?" she asked.

"Sure. It might be pouring tomorrow," said Danny. "We can take a bus. I'll phone Joe and tell him to meet us at the stop on the corner."

When they got on the bus, the driver raised his eyebrows at their vacuum cleaner. "We're just going to clean up the city," Joe remarked.

By bus, it was a short ride to Mr. Anguish's neighborhood. They got off, and as they walked toward the street where his house was, Joe said, "I've got a theory."

"About Mr. Anguish?" said Irene.

"Uh-huh. Suppose he's an international spy?"

Danny grinned. "That's some suppose. How did you decide that?"

"Well, he kept to himself most of the time. He had no friends. He leaves the house one morning and a little later a ragged man comes looking for him. That fellow we saw wearing old ragged clothes, the one who talked to him, could have been working with him. Maybe the clothes were a disguise. Maybe he came to warn Mr. Anguish that the FBI was on his tail, but he was too late. Because in the meantime, they had picked up Mr. Anguish. That's why he vanished."

"Wouldn't the police know about it?" Danny said.

Joe shook his head. "Nope. It would be too secret."

"Well, it's an idea," said Irene. "But what could a spy be doing in Frognall & Pounder's department store?"

"That's just it," Joe said triumphantly. "Nobody'd suspect him."

"He wouldn't find out anything he could use, either," Danny grunted. "It doesn't sound right to me. But here's the house. Let's try out Bleeper the Bloodhound first, and work out theories later."

As they approached the front steps, Irene said in a low voice, "There's someone inside."

Dan had been about to turn on the machine. He hesitated. "How do you know?"

"Look at that window, the one on the porch. You can see the curtain move."

Even as Danny looked, the curtain was pulled aside. A white-haired woman stared out at them. She frowned and flapped her hand, motioning them to go away.

"It's his housekeeper," Danny said. "She must have come back."

"What'll we do?" said Joe.

"Just what we were going to do," said Danny stubbornly. "We won't bother her."

He threw the switch, and began moving the nozzle back and forth slowly along the bottom step. Almost at once, it began to give out a rapid series of high-pitched bleeps.

"It works!" Irene cried.

"That woman's still scowling at us, and waving," said Joe nervously. "Let's go."

97

Danny was already moving down the street, following the bleeps as the machine's sensitive panels picked up and identified Mr. Anguish's smell.

The robot bloodhound led them into a street of larger, more expensive houses, and then down a slight hill to a green square where a statue of a World War I soldier stood with his rifle at the ready, looking dauntlessly into the distance. The trail then turned left along a wide avenue leading toward the business district. There were more people, and

shops began to appear, and from time to time
the bleeps would grow fainter as the trail
faded among all the other smells which over-
lay it. The friends were taking turns at carrying the machine, which was heavier than they
had expected, and whoever was operating it
had to swing the nozzle back and forth until it
picked up the right scent again. Passers-by
stared at them in surprise, and one man said,
"Hey, kids, looking for buried treasure?"

"No," Joe retorted. "There's a sunken
ship somewhere around here."

At last, they turned into Main Street. The trail was now harder to follow than ever, and they had to go very slowly. They crossed a street called Glenn Road, and Joe pointed to a store on the corner.

"That must be the shop he went into to buy cigars," he said.

"Right," said Danny. "It's only four blocks more to The Frog Pond. Somewhere between here and there, he vanished."

The trail continued to the next corner, where a narrow street of old, low, brick buildings joined Main Street. Irene was carrying the bloodhound, making wide sweeps with the nozzle. *Bleep!* it went at one end of the sweep, and then, suddenly, *bleep-bleep!* at the other.

"That's funny," she said. "It sounds as if he went in two directions."

"Try it again," said Danny. "Swing it over that way, first, and then the other way."

Obediently, she did so. The bloodhound bleeped in both places.

"One way goes across the street, I think," said Joe. "And the other one around the corner and up this narrow street."

100

Danny considered the matter with a frown. Then his face cleared. "I know! That way, across the street, is the way he went every day to the store. You can hear that the signal isn't quite as strong; that's because it's older. *This* way, around the corner, must have been the way he went day before yesterday, the day he disappeared."

Irene nodded. Holding the nozzle close to the ground, she began to follow the trail that led into the side street. The boys pressed eagerly beside her. The signals were faint but clear. On they went, almost to the center of the block. And then, abruptly, the bleeps stopped.

They gazed at each other in surprise. Irene moved about, snapping the switch on and off, but beyond a certain point there was no further sound.

"Is there something wrong with it?" asked Joe.

"No, of course not," said Danny. "It works all right when we backtrack. It just stops here."

"Then this is the spot where he vanished," Irene said. "It's *got* to be. But—" She looked around. They were at a point where the walls of two office buildings met, and the nearest doorway was some distance away. "But where did he go?" she finished helplessly.

"Straight up?" said Joe. "A helicopter came down between the—no, I guess not."

"He couldn't have just gone out— pfft!—like a candle," Irene protested. "What *could* have happened to him?"

"There is one possibility," Danny began.

Before he could continue, a car pulled up alongside them and stopped. "What are you up to this time?" said a deep voice. "There are no ghosts in the middle of Spring Street."

"Hello, Mr. Ellison," Danny said, as the detective leaned out of the car window. "Not ghosts. We're tracking Mr. Anguish."

"Tracking him? With a vacuum cleaner?" Mr. Ellison sounded confused.

"It's not a vacuum cleaner," Danny said. "It's a robot bloodhound."

Mr. Ellison pushed his hat back. "You interest me strangely," he said. "Go on. You'd better explain."

102

Danny told him how the machine worked, and how they had followed Mr. Anguish's scent to this spot.

"Well, well. You put that thing together yourselves?" Mr. Ellison said, in admiration. "I have to admit, you're quite a team. And you were actually able to track Anguish to here?"

"That's right," said Danny.

Mr. Ellison looked about, just as they had done. "Short of him having flown away like a sparrow, I don't see how it could have happened. Are you sure there isn't something wrong with your machine?"

"I don't think so. There *is* something he could have done that would make his trail end here."

"What's that?"

"He could have stepped into a car," Danny said.

Mr. Ellison looked solemnly at the boy for a long moment. Then he carefully opened the car door and swung himself around so that his feet rested on the pavement. That way, he was more comfortable. He folded his arms deliberately.

"Daniel," he said, "you are a pretty smart kid. Go ahead. Got any more ideas?"

"Yes, sir," said Danny. "A theory about why Mr. Anguish would have gotten into a car. Maybe he was dragged into one."

"Um-hm. Kidnapped, you mean? But why?"

"Well . . ." Danny glanced at his friends. "Don't you remember," he said to them, "when we went to Mr. Anguish's office with the Professor, and he said something important about the lock?"

They shook their heads. "He said a lot of things," said Irene. "Which do you mean?"

"He said that the lock would only operate with the right key. And the key—"

"I remember now," said Joe. "The key was Mr. Anguish's hand."

"Yes," said Danny, "so maybe somebody kidnapped him to get the key to the safe."

"Very good thinking," said Mr. Ellison. "V-e-r-y good. Now, since you're so bright, maybe you can tell me what happened this morning."

Danny grinned widely, beginning to say,

"How could I—?" A second look at Mr. Ellison's face sobered him.

"The safe!" he exclaimed suddenly. "You don't mean—"

"That's what I do mean," Mr. Ellison said grimly. "This morning, the department store safe was burgled."

EIGHT

More Theories

"Get into the car," Mr. Ellison said. "We'll be a bit more private, that way."

The three, still stunned from his news, bundled themselves and their machine into the back seat of the big car. Mr. Ellison swung around in his seat so that he could look at them.

"Now, Dan," he said, in a serious tone, "we'd better talk this over."

"Yes, sir. What do you want to talk about?"

Mr. Ellison eyed him for a moment. His gaze went to Irene and Joe, who looked as pale and startled as Danny.

Then he said, "Did you really work that all out by yourself? About Mr. Anguish being kidnapped because his hand was the key to the safe?"

"Of course I did," said Danny. "Why?"

"And the bit about him being dragged into a car? That vacuum cleaner of yours really works?"

"Sure it does."

"And we told you, it's not a vacuum cleaner," put in Irene.

"No. I'm sorry. That piece of information is useful. It provides a clue which I'll have to check out. Now, I want you to tell me something, straight."

"What?" Danny asked.

"Where *is* Professor Bullfinch?"

Danny reddened. "So you've found out he's not registered at the hotel. Well, I don't know where he is. Neither does my mother."

"Honestly?"

"Cross my heart."

After another long look at him, the

detective grinned. "All right, don't look so worried, I believe you. But I may as well tell you that I was on my way to your house when I caught sight of you down this street. You see, we had already come to the same conclusion—that Mr. Anguish was kidnapped so that he could be used to open the safe. Detective Sergeant Macedo thinks that Professor Bullfinch may have had something to do with it."

"What?" Danny burst out.

"He couldn't have," said Irene. "That's ridiculous."

"Impossible," Joe added. "If you knew the Professor—"

"But I don't," said Mr. Ellison. "And when you've been in the business of solving crimes as long as I have, you know that nothing is impossible. I'd have said it was impossible for Mr. Anguish to vanish in the middle of a street, but you've just shown me how it could have happened. Isn't that so?"

The three were silent.

"In fact," Mr. Ellison said, "it made me suspect that maybe you knew something you weren't telling me. But we'll skip that, now."

Danny drew a breath. "When did the robbery happen?"

"There was a big special sale yesterday, and the store was open until nine at night. The money was put in the safe and locked away by Mr. String. This morning, when he came to the office and opened the safe, he found it empty."

He took out a long, thin cigar, glanced from it to the young people, and put it back in his pocket. "You've met that fellow, String, haven't you?" he said. "Would you say he liked Mr. Anguish?"

"No, he didn't," said Danny. "I saw the way he looked at him. He thought Mr. Anguish was putting too many improvements into the store."

"Uh-huh. And you know, Mr. String worked there for thirty-seven years, and when old Mr. Frognall died and his nephew, Mr. Chambers, took over, Mr. Anguish was hired as manager. Mr. Chambers thought that Mr. String was out of date. I don't blame him for feeling bitter. A funny guy," he mused. "He's been cooperative, but he won't tell us where he was between eight-thirty and nine on the morning of Mr. Anguish's disappearance."

"He won't?" Irene said. "Isn't that suspicious? Are you going to arrest him?"

"Oh, we don't arrest people that quickly," said Mr. Ellison. "We're keeping an eye on him. And we're still looking everywhere for traces of Mr. Anguish. I went to his house a few hours ago. His housekeeper had just returned, and she let us search the place, but there's no hint of where he went. He didn't take a suitcase or any clothes, not even a comb or razor, so it looks as if whatever happened to him was unexpected. He didn't go away voluntarily."

"We saw the housekeeper," said Danny. "A white-haired woman?"

"That's her."

"She chased us away."

"I'm not surprised. I suppose she doesn't want to be pestered by busybodies—the kind of people who gather around and stare when anything like this happens. Don't you kids go making nuisances of yourselves."

"We won't."

"Now, listen. I've been very open and

110

friendly with you," Mr. Ellison continued. "I want you to do something for me."

"Okay. What?" Danny said.

"I want you to let me know the minute you hear from Professor Bullfinch." He took out a card. "Here's a phone number where you can reach me. If I'm not there, they'll get the message to me. Will you do it, even though you think I'm wrong about the Professor?"

Danny took the card. "All right," he said. "If you'll promise not to do anything that'll hurt Professor Bullfinch."

"If the Professor hasn't done anything wrong, he has nothing to worry about from me," said Mr. Ellison earnestly.

Danny put the card in his pocket.

"One more thing," Mr. Ellison said. "You youngsters seem to know all about this science stuff, particularly the lock the Professor put on the store safe. Is that right?"

"Why, yes," Danny said. "That is—I mean—well, we don't know *all* about it."

"I'll go a step further—I don't know *anything* about it," said Joe.

"Will it work if the hand that's put into it is—" Mr. Ellison paused, and then finished ominously, "—cold?"

"Cold? In August?" Danny said, in puzzlement.

Irene gasped. "I know what he means," she said. "He means, dead."

"That's right, Irene," said Mr. Ellison. "We're afraid that whoever kidnapped Mr. Anguish may have killed him if he refused to help them open the safe. In fact, even if he cooperated with them, they may have killed him afterward so that he couldn't identify them."

Danny found it hard to speak. "I—I don't think it would work if he was dead. But I don't know for sure."

"Okay, never mind," said Mr. Ellison.

"Can I ask you something?" Danny said.

"I'll answer as long as it's not an official secret."

"About Mr. String. When he came to work did he walk, like Mr. Anguish, or did he take a bus, or what?"

Mr. Ellison raised his eyebrows. "That's an odd question. Why do you want to know?"

"Oh, just an idea. But if you don't want to tell me—"

"It's okay. He drove in his own car. Now, can you tell me why you want to know?"

Danny squirmed. "Not yet. I want to think about something."

Mr. Ellison shrugged. "All right. I won't press you. Now, as long as you're in the car, where can I drop you?"

Before the others could speak, Danny said quickly, "Oh, just let us out here, thanks. We're going to—uh—stroll around."

His friends knew at once that he had some sort of plan in mind, and said nothing.

"If you say so," said Mr. Ellison, opening the car door. "Remember, let me know if you hear anything at all about where the Professor is."

"I will."

When the detective had driven off, Irene said, "What's up, Danny?"

Danny squinched up his freckled nose. "Nothing's really up. But I was wondering whether we could find out if Mr. String had anything to do with Mr. Anguish's disappearance."

"But why?" said Irene. "Why would Mr. String have to use Mr. Anguish as a key? *He* could open the—"

She stopped in mid-sentence. "Oh," she said. "I see."

"I don't," said Joe.

"Suppose Mr. Anguish found out that Mr. String was planning to rob the safe," Irene explained. "Then Mr. String would

114

have to kidnap him to keep him from telling the police."

"I get it. And then String would report that Anguish was missing," Joe said. "That would keep them from suspecting him. But if *he* kidnapped Mr. Anguish three days ago, then the chances are that poor old Anguish is—"

Danny nodded. "Finished. Right. It would be the safest way for Mr. String to keep him quiet."

"So that's why you asked Mr. Ellison how Mr. String went to work," Irene said. "You were thinking of Mr. String getting Mr. Anguish into his car, driving him away somewhere and tying him up—ooh, how awful! Do you really think Mr. String would do such a thing?"

"He looked sour enough for anything," said Danny. "And you didn't see the nasty look he gave Mr. Anguish. Listen, we're not far from The Frog Pond, and we've got Bleeper the Bloodhound with us. If we can find out where Mr. String parks his car, all we have to do is get into it and see whether there's any trace of Mr. Anguish's scent."

115

"Sounds simple," said Joe. "Let's get going. It's getting late."

They made their way to the department store, Joe and Irene lugging Bleeper between them, and Danny holding the nozzle. When they got there, Irene said, "You two wait out here. We can't go marching through the store carrying what looks like a vacuum cleaner. They'll think we stole it. I'll go in and see if I can find out where Mr. String leaves his car."

"Try not to take too long," said Danny. "It must be nearly closing time."

They waited near the door, pushing Bleeper up against the wall and standing in front of it so as not to attract any attention. In a surprisingly short time, Irene was back. She looked flustered.

"You'll never guess who I saw in there," she said.

"Not Mr. Anguish?"

"No. That ragged young man. The one we saw outside Mr. Anguish's office. He's standing near one of the counters."

"What'll we do?" said Joe. "Arrest him? Trip him and knock him flat? Call the cops?"

"Calm down," Danny said. "Never mind him for a minute. What about Mr. String's car?"

"Oh, that. It was easy." Irene mopped her damp face with her handkerchief. "I went up to the Information Desk and asked if there was a parking lot connected with the store, because my Dad said he was going to meet me there. The woman said it was around in back of the store, on Jackson Street. If it belongs to the store, you can be sure that's where Mr. String parks."

"That's right. Good work, Irene. Now, let's see. What would be best to do?" Danny asked.

"This," said Irene. "You and Joe go ahead with the plan. Find Mr. String's car and try Bleeper in it. Then wait around at the lot for me. I'll go inside and keep an eye on the ragged man."

"What if he goes out?" Joe asked.

"Then," Irene said boldly, "I'll follow him."

Dan scratched his head. "I don't know," he said. "Suppose he sees you? He might get rough."

"If he sees me, he isn't going to think anything about a girl walking behind him. And if the worst comes to the worst—I'll run."

"That," said Joe, with a sigh, "is what I'd like to do right now."

NINE

The Ragged Man

Irene had spoken more bravely than she actually felt. But she made herself walk back into the crowded store, and then began looking for a good position from which to watch her quarry.

He wore the same tattered army jacket, blue jeans with ragged bottoms, and a sweat shirt with a faded picture of Snoopy in a flier's helmet. His long hair was tied back today in a ponytail like Irene's, and his beard had been trimmed to a point. He looked very hippie-ish, but Irene agreed with what Danny had once said—to the eyes of Mr. Anguish's neighbor he would seem to be a tramp.

He was lurking near the perfume counter, not far from the elevators. Beside the elevators there was a bench, and Irene found that sitting there she could keep him in view while managing to look as if she were waiting for someone.

For a time, the ragged man stood perfectly still, watching the customers who came to the counter. After a while, he took out a tiny notebook in a secretive kind of way, jotted something in it, and tucked it away again. With his hands in his pockets, he wandered over to the counter where jewelry was on display. Once again, he watched the customers and then wrote something in his notebook.

"What's he up to?" Irene thought.

Suddenly, she understood. Every time a clerk rang up a sale, the ragged young man furtively craned his neck to see how much it was. These figures were what he seemed to be noting down. "Of course!" she told herself. "He wants to see how much money they're making. He *must* have had something to do with the robbery."

The man began looking about him with a frown. He seemed uneasy, as if he had become aware that someone was watching him. Shoving his notebook into his pocket, he turned and strode away. His movement was so abrupt that Irene almost lost him. With a squeak of dismay, she jumped up. She was in time to see him going along an aisle between pocketbooks and belts.

She tore after him, dodging around shoppers or squeezing between them. As she turned a corner, she ran full tilt into a man whose arms were full of parcels. He staggered backward into a woman carrying a shopping bag, and for a moment the air was full of packages.

"Sorry!" Irene gasped. The ragged man was just leaving the store by a side door. She didn't wait to apologize any further or to see what was happening behind her, but dashed off in pursuit of him.

When she emerged into the street, the ragged man was far ahead, walking briskly in

121

the opposite direction from Main Street. Irene trotted after him, and when she had come to within a dozen yards of him matched her pace to his. At Jackson Street, he crossed without waiting for the light, in spite of the traffic. Irene hovered on the corner while a truck went past and saw him stop and look behind him. She tried to appear as innocent as she could, rolling up her eyes and puckering her lips in a whistle, but it seemed to her that his gaze rested on her for a moment. Did he suspect anything?

He was off again, and she skipped across in front of a car which jammed on its brakes and blew its horn angrily at her. "Sorry," she muttered again automatically.

The ragged man was walking faster. There was no doubt of it, now—he knew she was after him, for he kept glancing back over his shoulder.

"Oh, dear," Irene said to herself. "Now, what? Maybe I'd better stop following him. Maybe we should have told Mr. Ellison about him. Maybe—"

And then she saw that he was gone. There were one or two other people on the pavement ahead, but no sign of the ragged man.

"Everybody disappears!" She all but said it aloud. A shiver ran up her spine. Perhaps this was some sort of curious power shared by a secret society—a group of people who could become invisible at will? "Nonsense, Irene!" she told herself sternly. "He's probably just gone into one of those buildings."

123

She started off again up the street. She went more slowly, now, unsure how she was to find him and still debating within herself whether to go on trying to follow him after all. Halfway along, there was a space between two buildings, a kind of narrow little alleyway. Because she was going more deliberately, Irene saw it before she came to it. A warning thrill prickled the hairs on her neck and she halted.

Now she could see a tiny hint of brown cloth showing at the edge of the nearer building. She began to back away, and as she did so the man stuck his head out for a quick peep. She turned and fled.

She heard his footsteps on the sidewalk behind her. She knew he could catch up with her because his legs were longer than hers. In desperation, she whirled in her tracks. He was galloping toward her with a scowl on his face. She ran right at him, and before he could stop himself or reach for her, she had shot past him and was off in the opposite direction.

When she came to the alleyway, she darted into it. She had a confused thought that

she might find a back door she could get into, or perhaps the alley might lead to another street where she could find a policeman.

To her horror, it ended in a high brick wall. She spun around with her back to the wall to face her pursuer. Her breath burned in her throat so that she could barely speak.

"Don't you—don't you dare do anything!" she panted.

He had stopped a few steps off and was glowering angrily at her.

"All right, man, like, what's it all about?" he said.

"You know what it's about," Irene retorted. "You'd better leave me alone or I'll scream for the cops."

"Wild!" said the ragged man. "*You'll* scream for the cops? What do you think I'm going to do?"

Irene glared. "I don't know what you think you're *going* to do," she said stoutly. "What have you done with Mr. Anguish?"

"What have I done with Mr. Who?"

"Don't try to pretend you don't know him. We all saw you talking to him in the store the other day."

The man stared at the walls on either side of him, and at last cast his eyes upward at the strip of cloudy sky above the alley. "Man!" he cried. "You're really freaked out. I don't know anybody in the—"

He paused. "In the store?" he repeated. "Wait a minute. I do know that name."

He fumbled through his pockets and finally brought out a scrap of paper.

"Anguish," he said, scanning it. "Right on. He's the manager of the store."

"Well, of course he is," Irene faltered. Both her fear and her certainty were beginning to ooze out of her. "And you *were* talking to him. I remember that you showed him something."

The ragged man began to grin. Suddenly, he no longer looked either sinister or threatening.

"Sure," he agreed. "This."

He reached into a back pocket, pulled out a wallet, and from it took a small card which he handed to her. A little shakily, she took it. It had his picture on it, and the words,

*This identifies Harold Spillett as a
student of Midston University.*

"Oh," said Irene.

"I'm studying the psychology of merchandising," he went on. "That is, what makes people flock into big stores, what makes them buy things, and all that jazz. I had to get permission from Anguish to hang around and observe, so they wouldn't think I was a shoplifter or something. You dig?"

"I dig," said Irene, in a very small voice.

127

Mr. String's Secret

Danny and Joe found the parking lot easily.
It was in a large open space surrounded by a
high wire fence, at the entrance to which was
a sign that said parking was free to customers
of Frognall & Pounder's. A sleepy-looking
man wearing a denim jacket sat tilted back in
a chair before a tiny shack inside the gate.

"We've got quite a choice," Joe said.
"How are we going to find Mr. String's car?
Go around looking for his initials on it?"

"Not as complicated as that," replied Danny, "Just follow me and don't say anything crazy."

He marched up to the guard. "Excuse me," he said politely. "Mr. String asked us to put this vacuum cleaner in his car. Which one is it?"

The guard yawned. "Down at the end of the lot. Blue Ford. You'll see his name on the wall behind it."

He closed his eyes again. Danny winked at Joe, and they made their way to the far side of the lot between the ranks of cars. They found Mr. String's Ford without trouble. Joe opened the door and between them they hauled Bleeper into the back. Danny was just getting the nozzle into a position from which he could pass it over the front seat as well as the back one, when Joe caught hold of his wrist.

"We've got to get out of here!" Joe whispered. "Here comes String."

But a glance told them it was already too late.

"He'll see us," Danny said. "And if the guard told him what we said, he'll start asking questions. Pull the door shut and crouch down on the floor."

"I don't—" Joe began, but Danny was already flat on the floor in the back with Bleeper. Joe closed the door and folded himself down next to his friend. There was a good bit of space between the back seat and the front, but even so it was a squash.

They huddled together, hardly daring to breathe. Danny was already thinking desperately, "Why do I always act so fast? Why don't I stop and count ten, first? We should have taken a chance and run. If the guard told Mr. String that two boys came to put a vacuum cleaner in his car, he'll certainly look for it. He'll look in the back here, and find us. What'll I say?"

Luckily, he didn't have to think up an excuse. The guard, half-asleep, had paid no attention to the familiar figure of the store's assistant manager. Mr. String settled himself behind the wheel, started the car, and pulled out of the lot.

The boys lay frozen, bracing themselves against the bumps and turns so that they wouldn't make any noise. They could hear a curious sound coming from the front seat, and after a moment realized that it was Mr. String humming to himself. After a bit, he began to sing in a cracked voice:

I'm sitting on top of the world,
Just singing a song,
Just rolling along . . .*

"Keep rolling along and don't look in the back seat," Danny prayed.

After what seemed like hours, but could only have been a few minutes, the car stopped. They felt the back of the seat push against them as Mr. String leaned over. He blew his horn.

After a second or two, someone on the sidewalk said, "Hiya, Doug."

"Sorry to make you come out," said Mr. String, "but I can't park here."

"What are you up to?" the voice said. "Did you close the store early?"

"No, Henry. I have to go to the doctor for an injection, and then I'm going back to close up. I just stopped to tell you that I can't make it tomorrow."

"Too bad. Did she find out about it?"

"No, she doesn't know anything. But we had some trouble at the store. You know about Anguish."

"You aren't sorry about *that,* eh?"

"No, but now I've got a detective breathing down my neck and I'm afraid he'll find out about our little secret."

The other person laughed—a fat, fruity laugh. "We wouldn't want that to happen, would we?"

"You can say that again. So I'll just stay away for a couple of days."

"Okay, I'll have everything ready for you whenever you get back."

"Good. See you later."

"So long, Doug."

Danny's face was only a few inches from Joe's. They opened their eyes wide at each other. Mr. String started the car again and their foreheads were banged together, but they managed not to utter a sound.

After another endless drive, the car stopped and Mr. String got out. They heard his footsteps receding. When they could no longer hear him, they sat up, wincing and moaning.

"My blood has stopped running altogether," Joe said, rubbing first one arm, then the other.

"Never mind that," said Danny. "Did you hear what he said? His little secret! Open that door and get out, while I try the bloodhound. Warn me if you see him coming back."

Joe got out, looking around to see where they were. The car was parked in a small lot behind a low glass and cement building, alongside the door of which were half a dozen brass plates bearing doctors' names. There was no one else about. Dan picked up the nozzle and snapped on the switch. He ran the end of the nozzle along the back seat. There was no sound. He lifted it and passed it over the front seat.

At once, it began to bleep hysterically.

"That's it!" said Danny. "There you are—that proves it. Mr. String's secret is that he kidnapped Mr. Anguish." He shut off the bloodhound. "Listen, Joe, go phone Mr. Ellison. Here's the card he gave me with his number on it. Tell him what we've found out."

"What about you? What are you going to do?"

"I'll stay with the car. Maybe I'll find out something else. He said that after he got his injection, he'd go back to the store, so I'll hitch a free ride with him. Tell Mr. Ellison to catch him at the parking lot."

Joe ran off a pace or two, and returned just as Danny was about to close the car door.

"What's the matter?" Danny asked.

"Nothing's the matter. Have you got a dime for the phone?"

Danny found one and handed it over. Then he lay as flat as he could, holding Bleeper to keep it from rattling around. The minutes stretched out endlessly. To pass the time, he thought over all he knew about the case, and reviewed the conversation he had overheard between Mr. String and the man named Henry. He began to see what might have happened.

His train of thought was broken by the assistant manager's return. Soon they were on their way back to the store, with Mr. String humming again in front, and Danny clenching his teeth and bracing himself on the floor, a harder job now that Joe was no longer there and there was more space. But at last, the car came to a halt. They were back in the parking lot.

Danny remained in hiding, while Mr. String got out of the car. Suddenly, Mr. Ellison's deep voice said, "Just a moment, Mr. String. I'd like a word with you."

At that, Dan struggled up and pushed the door open with such haste that he tumbled headlong out of the car. He got to his hands and knees. Mr. String stood flabbergasted, goggling first at him, then at Mr. Ellison. Behind the burly detective were Joe and Irene.

"What's going on?" stammered Mr. String. "What's that boy doing in my car?"

"Take it easy," said Mr. Ellison calmly. "We'll straighten everything out. But first, I think—"

Before he could continue, Danny interrupted. Scrambling to his feet, he pointed at Mr. String. "He kidnapped Mr. Anguish! That's where he was the other morning

136

between eight-thirty and nine—waiting in his car around the corner. He had a friend with him, a man named Henry, and when they saw Mr. Anguish at the corner of the street, they called him over and bundled him into the car. Our robot bloodhound picked up Mr. Anguish's scent in the front seat."

"Just a second," said Mr. String. His face had become very mottled.

But Danny plunged on. "I'll bet he did it because he was jealous of Mr. Anguish, and he wanted to show everybody that the new safe wasn't foolproof. He figured everybody would think Mr. Anguish was kidnapped by crooks. Then he himself took the money out of the safe. I don't think he meant to keep it—he gave it to his friend, Henry, to hold."

"How do you know all this?" Mr. Ellison put in.

"I heard him talking when I was in the back of the car. I heard Henry say that they weren't sorry about Mr. Anguish's disappearance. I heard Mr. String tell Henry that he was afraid you'd find out about their secret, and Henry said he'd have everything ready for him when he got back."

137

"Is that true?" Mr. Ellison demanded, turning to Mr. String.

Mr. String clutched at his forehead. His bony, dried-up face had gone from red to white, and he almost looked as though he were about to burst into tears. "It—it is and it isn't," he said.

"I just thought of something else," Danny said, carried away by excitement. "That ragged man—I'll bet he was Henry."

"No, he wasn't," said Irene.

They all looked at her. With a shrug of embarrassment, as she remembered what had happened, she went on, "He's a student at Midston University, studying why people buy things in big stores. He got permission from Mr. Anguish to study the store, but he was never at Mr. Anguish's house. That must have been a real tramp."

"Oh. You talked to him, then," Danny said.

"I sure did."

Mr. Ellison's lips twitched. "We can rule him out, then. But this other stuff—" He rounded on Mr. String. "You'd better start explaining that 'It is and it isn't.' This matter is serious."

"All right," said Mr. String. "I didn't want it to come out, but I see I'll have to tell you. The fact is, I'm supposed to be on a diet."

Mr. Ellison's jaw dropped. "What? This case is driving me nuts! What has your diet got to do with it?"

"Oh, my," said Mr. String. "You see, I'd begun to get a—well—a little potbelly. And my wife insisted that I go on a diet. So for breakfast every day, she gave me nothing but a single piece of dry toast and one cup of black coffee without sugar. Working in the office, I can't really start the day on an empty stomach, so I took to leaving the house a little earlier than usual, and stopping at my friend Henry Svensson's café for a real breakfast— bacon and eggs and all the rest of it. I didn't want my wife to find out—she can be very disagreeable—and I was afraid that if I told you it might somehow get to her ears. That," he finished, with a long sigh, "was my secret."

Danny could feel his face flaming. He

said, "But our machine did pick up Mr. Anguish's scent on the seat of your car. And he always walked to and from work."

"I don't know what you mean by picking up his scent," snapped Mr. String, who, now that he had confessed, had recovered his customary sharpness of manner. "We drove to the airport last week to meet Mr. Chambers, the owner of the store."

Mr. Ellison put his hands on his hips and stared at Danny. He appeared, to the boy, to be about ten feet tall and growing bigger every minute.

"Well, Danny—?" he said.

ELEVEN

A Last Chance

Danny was still smarting from the lecture Mr.
Ellison had given them, when he went to bed
that night. The detective had driven the
three young people home, after apologizing
to Mr. String, and on the way had read them
the riot act. He had pointed out that children
had no business getting underfoot in an
investigation, that they had acted in an irre-
sponsible and thoughtless way, that they had
made things very difficult for him in a case

141

which was already giving him headaches, and that they had wasted his time.

"The trouble is, you judged by appearances," he said. "You did it with me, the first time we met, right? Then, you let the words 'ragged man' fool you. And then you thought that because Mr. String was envious of Mr. Anguish, he must be a criminal. That's not the way a policeman works. We try to gather facts, not jump to conclusions."

The fact that he spoke calmly, without raising his voice or sounding angry, made it worse. The three said nothing to each other except "Good night." To add to Danny's gloom, it began to rain, and in the short time it took him to struggle from the car to his door with Bleeper, he was soaked.

Mrs. Dunn was too wise to question him, for she could see at once that something unpleasant must have happened. She simply told him to change into dry things, and gave him an especially good dinner. She waited patiently, and over dessert he told her everything that had happened.

She was not the kind of mother who

always says, "I told you so," but she did say, "Maybe Mr. Ellison was right, Dan."

"Maybe, but he was only partly right," Danny said stubbornly. "We did try to gather some facts. We just went about it the wrong way, I guess. But the police still think Professor Bullfinch had something to do with the crime. I know they're wrong and so do you. Aren't *they* jumping to conclusions?"

"Not really, dear. They have to suspect everybody. They just want to ask him some questions. And you must admit it's odd that we don't know where he is."

"It may not be as odd as we think," said Danny. "I'll bet there's a simple explanation. But if I can find out who kidnapped Mr. Anguish, it'll stop them bothering the Professor."

Mrs. Dunn got up to clear the table. "Well, just be careful, and try not to get into any more trouble than you can help."

In the morning, things looked a bit better. The rain had stopped, and the day was bright, cool, and ready to be used. While Dan was eating breakfast, Joe phoned and said he'd be over soon; a little later, Irene ran across from next door and she and Danny sat under the old lilac waiting for Joe.

"Mr. Ellison was really rough," she said. "I guess I hated it mostly because he's such a nice man. I suppose he was right, wasn't he?"

Danny stuck out his lower lip truculently. "That's what Mom said. But if we had told him about the ragged man, he'd have checked the guy out the same way, wouldn't he? And if I hadn't been in such a hurry about Mr. String—if I'd just kept quiet and gone and told Mr. Ellison what we heard—he'd have questioned him. I think he was just sore because we followed up a couple of leads that he didn't know about."

Irene said, "Hm!" in a surprised way. "I never thought about that. Could be."

Joe bicycled up the walk, and leaped from his bike with a flourish. Leaving it on the grass, he joined them.

"What about the scientific method this morning?" he asked.

"There's nothing wrong with the scientific method," Danny answered. "The whole
144

trouble was me. I'm always diving into things without stopping to think. And I'll tell you both something—this morning I was doing a lot of serious thinking. There are a couple of questions about this case that I'd like to know the answers to."

"Yes, captain," Joe said, stretching out full length with his hands under his head. "Have you discussed them with Detective Ellison?"

Danny flushed. "You can kid around," he said, "but just listen. Number one: when those people kidnapped Mr. Anguish, why did they do it in the morning?"

"The early bird gets the manager," Joe said lazily.

Irene, however, nodded. "I see what you mean. Mr. Anguish went home at about six. Why didn't they grab him then, when there were fewer people about?"

"Sure," said Danny. "And another thing. Why, when they snatched him, didn't they use him to open the safe right away, the same night? Why did they wait a couple of days?"

Joe, growing interested, sat up. "Well, if he refused to help them, it would take them

145

some time, wouldn't it? They'd have to threaten him and scare him—maybe starve him—"

"Possibly. But I'm still wondering about it," Danny said. "You'd think that the way they'd do it would be to go into his house, maybe at midnight, and drag him out, and take him right to the store and grab his hand and shove it into the watchdog lock—"

Irene's head snapped up. "How did they know about the lock?" she said. "It had to be somebody connected with the store, didn't it? Or else—oh, no!—it couldn't really have been the Professor, could it, Danny?"

"I know it wasn't him. A lot of people knew about the lock. It was even in the papers."

"That's right, I'd forgotten."

"Maybe it was one of the night watchmen," Joe said, drawing lines in the ground with a stick. "I saw a movie once in which the murderer turned out to be a policeman. The last person you'd think of, but of course he was only disguised as a cop. Hey! Maybe Mr. Ellison—? No, I guess not," he finished, with a shake of his head. "He's a real policeman."

146

"I'll tell you what I think," Irene began, and then said, "Danny!"

Danny was sitting as if turned to stone, mouth and eyes wide.

Irene nudged him. He didn't move.

"He's off again," Joe grumbled.

Irene was about to say something, but just then Dan leaped to his feet, almost braining himself on a low branch.

"I know!" he yelled. "Oh, my gosh! I just—I think—"

"What?" said Irene. "What are you talking about?"

Danny waved his arms helplessly, as if unable to go on. At length, he drew a couple of deep breaths and became quieter.

"I'm not going to tell you anything," he said positively. "If I'm wrong this time, there's no reason for you two to get into trouble. But I know I'm *not* wrong. Don't ask me anything. Just hang on. I'm going to make a phone call."

He rushed into the house. Irene and Joe gazed at each other in bafflement.

"He's got one of his brainstorms," Irene said.

"Whatever it is, it's going to get us into more trouble," said Joe. "I wish I'd had a bigger breakfast. I may end up in jail with nothing but bread and water."

Danny was back before long, with an expression of such serious determination that Irene said, "What's going on? Who did you phone?"

"Mr. Ellison will be here in a few minutes," Danny said. "I had a hard time talking him into it, but he finally agreed to give me one last chance."

"Won't you even give us a hint?" said Irene.

"Nope. That way, you can say you didn't know anything about it and you won't get scolded if it's a flop. So for once, you won't land in any trouble with me, Joe," he added, grinning.

He would say nothing else, and they had to be content. He went to the lab to fetch Bleeper the Bloodhound, and then he and his friends waited on the sidewalk in front of the house until Mr. Ellison's big car drove up.

The detective got out and helped them

stow Bleeper on the floor in back. Irene and Joe got in with it, and Danny sat in front.

"Okay," Mr. Ellison said. "This had better be good, boy, or the world won't be big enough for both of us."

Danny looked up into the detective's face. There was just enough of a hint of a smile there to make him relax.

"Oh!" he exclaimed. "I'm sorry. I forgot something. Wait a sec. I'll be right back."

He shot out of the car and around the house to the lab. He was back in a moment or two, cramming something into his pocket.

"Thanks. I'm ready now," he said.

"Where to, first?" asked Mr. Ellison.

"Mr. Anguish's house," said Danny.

Mr. Ellison started the car. "I'm afraid this is all a little too late," he said, as he drove. "The best we can hope for is to find his body. Early this morning, we got a phone call. Mr. Anguish's briefcase was picked up last night by a local boy. His mother called the police, thinking it had been lost."

"Where was it?" Danny said.

"There's a little patch of woods just

beyond Grove Street, a kind of park. It was there, under some bushes. We've got a team searching the area for his body, now."

Danny was silent for a moment or two, and then he murmured, half to himself, "Now I know why he got into that car."

"What?" Mr. Ellison sounded startled.

"I'll tell you later."

Mr. Ellison glanced sidelong at him, raising an eyebrow. "Okay," he said patiently. "Any word from Professor Bullfinch yet?"

"No," said Danny. "But I think I know what's happened."

"You want to tell me?"

"I can't, because I don't really know. But what I do know," he added, almost fiercely, "is that he didn't have anything to do with this crime."

"So you keep saying. We talked to the Washington police again this morning. They said they'd have word about him for us before noon today. So we'll all know by then, won't we?"

The car glided to a stop in front of Mr. Anguish's house. They got out, and Dan hurried ahead to knock at the door. They waited, and he knocked again, more loudly, but no one came.

"Let's try the back door," said Joe.

They started around the corner. On the porch of the house next door sat the gray little woman with her knitting, looking as though she hadn't moved since they last saw her.

"Nobody's home, dearie," she called to Danny. "Why, hello! You're the children who visited me the other day. Is that the man who gave you the note for Mr. Anguish?"

"Me?" said Mr. Ellison. "What's she talking about?"

"Never mind," Danny said hastily.

"Mr. Anguish still hasn't come back," the talkative woman went on. "And Mrs. Botter, the housekeeper, has gone shopping. I saw her go out not twenty minutes ago."

"Do you know where she does her shopping?" Danny asked.

"I don't know for certain, dearie. This morning she went off that way—" she waved her hand, "so I guess she went to the Colossal Supermarket. It's four or five blocks down, past the traffic light."

"Thank you," said Danny.

They returned to the car. "Now what?" said Mr. Ellison. "Do you want to wait for her, or go somewhere else?"

"There's one question I want to ask her," Danny said earnestly. "Can we try the supermarket?"

Mr. Ellison drove there and pulled up in front of the entrance. Irene got out first, and said doubtfully—for she had only seen the housekeeper for a moment through a window—"Is that her?"

Mr. Ellison had met her when he searched the house. He straightened, and said, "Yes, that's Mrs. Botter."

They saw a white-haired woman with glasses, wearing a coat and scarf despite the warm weather, just coming out of the doorway with a bag of groceries in her arms.

Danny started toward her. "I want to—" he began.

The woman glanced from him to the large form of Mr. Ellison looming behind him. She shrank back and looked from side to side in alarm. The automatic door had closed behind her, and she turned aside and ran through the other, back into the store.

"Just a minute! Wait!" called Mr. Ellison.

Through the plate glass window they could see her making her way up one of the aisles.

Mr. Ellison gave his head a shake. "We startled her."

"Let's go after her," Danny cried. "Come on!"

They burst into the supermarket, to the astonishment and dismay of the shoppers and clerks. The manager came bustling over, and Mr. Ellison flashed his badge. At the same time, Joe bellowed, "There she goes—in the soups!"

Danny pounded after her, people jumping from his path and scolding at him. As he drew near the housekeeper, she heaved her bag of groceries at him. It broke and sent a flood of eggs, corn flakes, and bread rolling under his feet. As he tried to avoid them, she vanished.

Joe and Irene had gone by way of the canned vegetables, hoping to head her off.

But she was already hurrying in the opposite direction, toward the frozen foods, shoving people out of her way. Dan and his friends met, at the end of the soup aisle, so suddenly that they could not stop and collided with a thump. They recovered, and went after her again at top speed.

Mr. Ellison, meanwhile, had hung back, watching the chase, waiting to see which way the woman would go. He now set off for the frozen foods, holding up his hand to stop her. She paused, seized a shopping cart full of groceries in spite of the loud protests of its owner, and with a shove sent it flying at the detective. He tried to sidestep, but it crashed into him. He stumbled and almost fell into the TV dinners.

The three young people appeared at the same time. The woman, cornered, snatched up a package of frozen spinach and hurled it at Joe, who was in the lead. He dodged. Mr. Ellison regained his balance and closed in.

"Hold it!" he commanded.

And at the same instant, Danny shouted, "Her glasses! Look at her glasses!"

The sunlight came pouring in through

the big front windows, striking at the wall along which the frozen foods were stored. It shone on the woman's face, and as they stared at her, her glasses darkened until her eyes could no longer be seen behind them.

"It's him," said Irene. "Mr. Anguish!"

Now, they recognized him, although his beard had been shaved off and he wore a wig and woman's clothing. He snarled at them. With his back against the case of frozen vegetables, he opened the handbag which still hung over his arm, took out a pistol, and leveled it at the three youngsters.

"Don't move," he said to Mr. Ellison. "Or I'll shoot one of the kids."

He glared at the detective, who stood motionless. In that instant, with Mr. Anguish's attention all on Mr. Ellison, Danny dragged something out of his back pocket. It looked like a gun—but when he pulled the trigger, a stream of white foam shot out.

It covered Mr. Anguish's face and began to stiffen. He dropped his weapon and clawed at the stuff. Danny shot still more of the plastic foam at him, covering his hands and arms and plastering his chest.

155

"Gug! Ung!" Mr. Anguish roared, locked in the hardened foam.

Mr. Ellison was already upon him, holding him fast.

"Get this stuff off him before he smothers," said the detective.

Irene and Dan quickly peeled away the material. Mr. Anguish's face appeared, red and twisted with fury. As soon as his hands were free, Mr. Ellison snapped a pair of handcuffs on him.

"And now," said the detective, "I think we'll go back to police headquarters and have a nice little talk."

TWELVE

The Triumph of the Scientific Method

The first thing Danny's eyes lighted on, when he walked into the gray-walled room at Police Headquarters, was Professor Bullfinch. The boy gave a glad cry and ran to seize the scientist by the hands.

"What are you doing here?" he said.

Professor Bullfinch looked both amused and bewildered. "I don't quite know," he replied. "I got off the Washington plane and was met by a police car, which brought me here. We've only just arrived."

There was another detective there, a short, broad-shouldered, stern-looking man. He said, "We'll get to that in a minute. What's this crowd you've brought in, Detective Ellison?"

"This is Danny Dunn, Sergeant Macedo. I've told you about him. These are his friends, Joe Pearson and Irene Miller. And this is the man we've been looking for, Stanley F. Anguish."

"Her? She's *him?*" said the sergeant. "If this is a joke—"

Mr. Ellison reached up and yanked the white wig off Mr. Anguish's head. Sergeant Macedo let out a long whistle.

"Good work, Ellison. Very good. So he's not dead or kidnapped after all. How did you figure it out?"

"I can't take the credit," Mr. Ellison said. "It was this boy. I still don't know how he guessed."

Sergeant Macedo fixed Danny with his sharp gaze. "All right, let's get to the bottom of this," he said gruffly. "Tell us how you did it, son."

Danny blushed and shrugged, a bit over-

159

awed by the detective's fierce manner. But Professor Bullfinch, smiling, said, "Please go on, Dan. I don't know what this is all about, but I think I can follow it."

Danny drew a deep breath. "It all came together for me over something Joe said," he began. "I'd been thinking about Mr. Anguish's disappearance, and the burglary, and there were some questions I couldn't find the answers for. A lot of things didn't make sense. Yesterday, Mr. Ellison scolded us for jumping to conclusions about Mr. String, and warned us against judging people by appearances. Then, this morning, Joe and Irene and I were talking, and Joe told us about a movie in which the crime was committed by a policeman. He said, 'It was the last person you'd think of, but he was only disguised as a cop.'"

"That's right, that's what I said," Joe put in. "But I don't see what it meant to you."

"What it meant," said Danny, "was that I started thinking, who is the last person we'd think of who might have burgled the safe? Why, the innocent victim, of course: Mr. Anguish. And then I thought—suppose he

160

disguised himself as his opposite, the way the crook in Joe's movie disguised himself as *his* opposite, a policeman? Okay, what's the opposite of a nice, neat, respectable store manager? A ragged tramp."

"What?" said Irene. "But the ragged man I followed—"

"That's not the one I mean," said Danny. "I mean the one who came prowling around Mr. Anguish's house the morning he disappeared. The one who was staggering and tripping, according to that talky lady next door. She thought he was drunk. She was judging by appearances, just the way everybody does. There's another reason, though, why somebody staggers around. If he's used to wearing glasses and then takes them off, he can't see so well."

"Well, I'll be—" said Sergeant Macedo, in a voice that was suddenly full of respect. "Good thinking, kid. Go on."

"There isn't much more," Danny said. "As soon as I saw that, everything else started to clear up and I could answer my questions."

"What were the questions?" asked Mr. Ellison.

161

"In the first place, if Mr. Anguish was kidnapped, why was it done in the morning on his way to work? And why did the kidnappers wait for a couple of days before robbing the safe? And also, what made Mr. Anguish change his regular routine that morning, go around the corner and halfway down the block, and then suddenly get into a car?

"I could figure out the answers to the first two questions. Mr. Anguish must have disguised himself somehow and gone home. He hid there, knowing everybody would think he'd been kidnapped. He waited for two reasons: one, because he knew the big sale was coming when there'd be a lot of money in the safe; and two, because everybody would be concentrating on looking for him and wouldn't think about a robbery. Then, later, they'd think he had been killed so they'd never suspect him of being the robber.

"But—" he turned to Mr. Ellison. "when you told me that his briefcase had been found in a patch of woods near Grove Street, I had the third answer and I knew I was right. One kind of car he would get into willingly was—a taxi."

"That's right, by gosh."

"So then I knew what he'd done. When he left home that morning, he had a dirty old cap in his briefcase. He walked his usual way, stopped and talked to the Professor—what did you say to him, by the way, Professor?"

"I asked him how the new safe was working out," Professor Bullfinch answered.

"That's what I figured. Then he went around the corner and hailed a taxi. He had the cab drive him to Grove Street, and he went into the woods and threw his hat away—"

"We found it," Sergeant Macedo said.

"—put on the old cap, turned his jacket inside out and ripped it a bit, tore some holes in his pants, took off his glasses, and walked home. Grove Street is only a few blocks from where he lives. He didn't want anyone to recognize him walking along the street and know that he'd come home. I suppose, after he bumped into the railing, he put his glasses on again for a minute, looked around and made sure nobody was watching—the nosy neighbor had gone in to phone the police— and then nipped quickly into the house."

"But how did you know he was disguised as a woman?" asked Sergeant Macedo.

"Oh, well, it was a case of opposites again," Danny replied. "Once he was in the house, he was safe, but he'd have to go out once in a while for groceries, and he couldn't avoid having lights on which the neighbors would see, just the way the neighbors noticed lights in that old house on Beckforth Street. He couldn't be a tramp anymore, so he chose another disguise, another opposite. A woman. He must have prepared for it by having a wig and women's clothes ready. He shaved off his beard as soon as he got home. He must have sent his housekeeper away and then everybody would just think she'd come back. Judging by appearances again, see? The housekeeper must have been white-haired and worn glasses, so if the neighbors saw a white-haired woman come out of the house, they'd just take it for granted it was her."

"When did you start to suspect that?" said Sergeant Macedo.

"I didn't really suspect. I just thought it was funny that when the woman chased us away, she didn't come out to see what we were doing, or what we wanted. Well, of course, Mr. Anguish had met us and was afraid we might know him in spite of his disguise. Then, later, when I worked things out, I wondered why the housekeeper had taken such a short vacation. Why did she come home so soon, and why did she stay there if Mr. Anguish was missing, maybe dead? The answer was that she wasn't the housekeeper, but Mr. Anguish himself."

Mr. Ellison looked bitterly at Mr. Anguish, who stood silent with his head hanging. "And he let me into the house and allowed me to look around, just as cool as you please. Of course, I'd only seen photographs of him, so I couldn't begin to recognize him." He turned to Danny. "You said you wanted to ask the housekeeper one question. What was it?"

"It wasn't anything," Danny said, with a

grin. "I just wanted to get close enough to sniff at her with Bleeper the Bloodhound. I was sure it would prove she was Mr. Anguish. But when we saw him at the supermarket, we hadn't yet had a chance to take the machine out of the car. It's a lucky thing I brought the foam gun. I just had a feeling we might need it."

"Bleeper the what?" said Professor Bull-finch.

"We converted your watchdog lock into a portable sniffer, and used the spare tape of Mr. Anguish's smell pattern to track him," Danny explained.

"That reminds me," said Sergeant Macedo. "We've been looking high and low for you, Professor. We thought you might have had something to do with the burglary. I'm sorry about that. I apologize. That's why, when the Washington police phoned and said you'd be on that plane, we went to meet you."

"Where were you?" Irene said. "Everybody was worried. Everybody of *us*, I mean," she added, darting a glance at the policemen.

"I never had a chance to register at my hotel," said the Professor. "Dr. Grimes met me at the airport and whisked me away to a top-secret conference. And for the next five days we—there were several other scientists there—stayed together and not a word of where we were was allowed to get out. I'm afraid I can't tell you any more than that."

"I'll bet it had something to do with your watchdog lock," Danny said.

The Professor merely smiled.

Sergeant Macedo went up to Mr. Anguish. "You've heard all this," he said. "Have you got anything to say before I book you?"

Mr. Anguish raised his shoulders and let them drop in a hopeless way. He said, "It all happened the way the boy says."

"You planned this some time ago, didn't you?" the detective asked.

"Yes. You see, Mrs. Botter, who kept house for me, is my sister. She has a son who got into serious trouble some time ago—he stole a car and cracked it up, damaging another car as well and injuring the driver. A lot of money had to be paid and neither she nor I had any way of getting it. So I thought of this scheme."

"Getting the Professor to develop a special lock for the safe?"

"Yes. Since I wanted the lock installed, nobody would suspect me of being the thief. I planned to reappear a day or two after the robbery with a story about having been kidnapped and kept prisoner until the thieves got out of the country. I was going to describe them, and I had a place all ready, a deserted shack way out in the woods where I was going to say they kept me.

"I was in the house when the children first came there. I saw them from an upstairs window, but I didn't imagine they suspected anything. I wish I had."

He raised his head. "My sister knows nothing about the plan. She's completely innocent. I sent her away, back to New Jersey where she has a little place of her own, telling her that I didn't need a housekeeper any longer and that I'd find the money for her somehow. The money is in my house, in the bureau in my bedroom." He sighed, and added, "I never dreamed anyone would discover me. I still don't know how the boy did it."

"It was the scientific method," Danny muttered.

"I don't know what method you used, but it worked," said Sergeant Macedo. "Detective Ellison, I think we owe this kid something, don't you?"

"I think he ought to be a member of the force," Mr. Ellison said.

"Right." Sergeant Macedo went to a desk, pulled open a drawer, and took out a gleaming gold badge. He pinned it on Danny's shirt. Like Mr. Ellison's badge, it bore the words, *Detective. Midston Police Department.*

"There," he said. "I've known worse detectives in my day. There'll be something more substantial than that, too, because Mr. Chambers, the owner of the store, has offered a reward for information leading to the capture of the robber and the return of the money."

Professor Bullfinch had been listening,

with an air of great attention, to everything that was said. He took out his pipe and began to fill it, chuckling.

"There's just one thing, Dan," he said. "A moment ago, you said you used the scientific method. I don't quite see how. You had no real hypothesis based on observation, to begin with, and as far as I can make out, you kept suspecting the wrong people and following false trails. You used excellent logic and common sense, but I don't think you can call it the scientific method, exactly."

"Sure it was, Professor," said Danny. "From my observations of you, I started with the hypothesis that you were innocent. And then I gathered as many facts as I could to prove it."

"You win," Professor Bullfinch said, with a smile.

Irene had been watching Mr. Anguish. "I know he's guilty," she said, "but I can't help feeling sorry for him."

"Me, too," said Danny. "I hope they won't be too tough on him."

"Thank you," Mr. Anguish said. "But

I'm glad it's ended like this. I haven't known a moment's real peace since I first planned it."

Professor Bullfinch rose and put an arm around Danny's shoulders. "My own hypothesis, based on my observations of young people, is that you must all be starving," he said. "So, if these gentlemen don't need us any longer, I propose to take you three out to lunch, including the biggest chocolate sundaes we can find."

Joe gave a sigh. "If that's the result of the scientific method, Professor," he said, as he followed the others out, "I hope you never stop using it."